I0543331

THE WHITFIELD RANCHER BOOK 1

KATHI S. BARTON

This is a work of fiction. Names, characters, places, and incidents are products of the author's imagination or are used fictitiously and are not to be construed as real. Any resemblance to actual events, locations, organizations, or persons, living or dead, is entirely coincidental.

World Castle Publishing, LLC
Pensacola, Florida
Copyright © Kathi S. Barton 2017
Paperback ISBN: 9781629896571
eBook ISBN: 9781629896588
First Edition World Castle Publishing, LLC, April 17, 2017
http://www.worldcastlepublishing.com
Licensing Notes
All rights reserved. No part of this book may be used or reproduced in any manner whatsoever without written permission, except in the case of brief quotations embodied in articles and reviews.
Cover: Karen Fuller
Editor: Maxine Bringenberg

CHAPTER 1

The hay baler was working the last two rows when Evan saw his dad riding his big bay horse toward him. Blake and Adrian, two of his brothers, had already been cut loose, and he was fixing to do the same to Joshua and David, his other brothers. He and Adam could handle this last bit, so he told them to head on back to the house before Dad got there.

"He looks like he's got something on his mind. I'm betting it has something to do with that trip he made today. It's not like him to go to town unless one of us is with him." Nodding at Adam, Evan watched as Dad dismounted and made his way toward them. "Are you staying for supper tonight, or heading back to town?"

"Town. I have to work in the morning." Dad asked him if they were about done. "Yes, sir. Adam and I are going to see to this before we put the tractor in the barn. Adrian said he'd clean it for me after supper."

"You not staying?" He told him the same thing he'd told Adam. "I don't know why you don't just quit that job. I know that you're good at it and all, but I'd sure like to see you more

5

than once a week, and that has you rushing off again. Come home, son. For good."

There was a bite to his voice, as if he was really pissed at him. Evan let out a long breath, picking up the next bale. Whatever was bothering his dad, he was sure it had nothing to do with his job.

"Dad, I'm thirty minutes away. Less if I need to hurry. And me working was what I went to college for. And I love what I do. It's rewarding to see how my job is making a difference. You know as well as I do that you have more than enough hands around if you need them." His dad nodded, but didn't say anything else. "Everything all right?"

"Yes. Why wouldn't it be?" Evan only shrugged. His dad was in a mood, and while it wouldn't last long, he could be a bear until it was over. "Your grandpa is coming for a visit. I guess he went and talked to your mom and they set it up. I was in town earlier picking him up. He's staying."

"You don't want him here?" His dad glared at him. "Maybe this would go better and a good deal faster if you were to tell me what burr you have up your butt. I'm not being disrespectful, but you're like a bear with his foot in a trap."

"I'm sorry, son. I love my dad. But he's a hog." Evan asked him what that was supposed to mean. "He wants to be in the middle of every little thing. He'll want to plan a big dinner and all the foods for it. Have you boys at his beck and call. I can't even get you to stay for supper."

"You didn't ask." His dad asked him then. He didn't sound so sour about it, but there was a tone that Evan decided to ignore. "I'd love to. But if I do, then you're going to tell me the real reason that you're ticked off. I know that you're not all that upset about Grandpa coming around. You love him as much as I do you."

"He wants to go over his will." Well, that was something. No one liked to be made to realize that they were as mortal as the next. "I'm not ready for that. I just.... We just buried my mom, and I don't want to talk about him leaving too. It's too much. But when I said that to your mother, she got all huffy with me."

"She got huffy or you got huffy?" His dad said he might have started it. "Mom loved Grandma too. I'm betting she no more wants to do this than you do. But I can also understand why Grandpa wants to do this. It was a mess when Grandma died, and she had everything all written out for the funeral director and all."

"No will was properly made out. I know that, I surely do, but it's just too soon. What am I gonna do if something happens to him too?" Evan hugged his dad and told him he had them. "Yes, but he's my dad. And...well, I don't know what I'm going to do. You know? He's always been there, him and Mom. And to think that he's making these plans...well, it just breaks my heart. Upsets me so that I get angry about it. I'm sorry, I am, but he's my dad."

"Maybe if you just let him do this, then he'll start to get better. You know as well as I that he's been in a bad way. Not that I blame him. I know that I would be as well. But if he feels like things are settled, then perhaps he'll start to come out of this depression a little more." His dad said nothing. "Dad, I don't know what else to say. He's going to do it, no matter what we try to say."

"What if he's doing this because he has plans to join Mom?

I mean, like right now, instead of waiting until his time comes along? I'm afraid, Evan, that is just what he's planning to do. This might be his way of getting things settled, as you called it, before he does something really stupid." Evan had actually thought of that but didn't want to mention it to his dad. "I can't lose another parent. Even as old as I am and knowing that he's getting up there, I just can't lose him."

"Neither can we. Neither can any of us." He hugged his dad, just held him while he got himself under control. Evan didn't know what he'd do if he lost any more of his family. They were the world to him.

Adam had moved away and was sitting in the truck, dealing with his own kind of grief. Losing Grandma had hit them all hard. She'd been the rock of the family. And she was going to be sorely missed.

There were still a few rows to go, so Evan asked his dad if he'd help. "Once we get this done, we won't have to worry about the rain until next season. And I, for one, would love to have this part of the end of season finished up."

"All right." They worked side by side, putting the bales of straw up on the truck bed as it slid out of the baler. It was hard work, but it felt good to be out in the sunshine. His dad, even as old as he was, did as good a job as Evan was doing keeping up with the machine as it made short work of the hay. And when they hit the last row, both climbed up on the bales and rode home that way. "I think I needed this too. Just to be able to think about nothing else for a time."

"It's one of the reasons I come home. To get away from the city, run a bit with my brothers, and to see you guys. It clears the mind." His dad nodded. "We'll talk to Grandpa, Dad.

Maybe if we show him how much we need him around, he'll rethink whatever it is he's got going on in his head."

"I'd like that too. I know you have to go back to work tomorrow, but I wish you'd reconsider coming home for good. It's not like you need the money, Evan. I really miss you. And I know that your brothers and mom do as well." Evan remained quiet, as there was nothing for him to say. He had to work or he'd go nuts. "You think on it. Maybe you can take some vacation time and see what you're missing here."

"I know what I'm missing. I think about it every day." They got off the hay and helped the hands put it in the barn. In a few weeks they'd have to go to the other field to do the same thing there, but for now they had enough to keep the few cows they had and the horses fed in the colder months. Plus, to sell to the other ranchers around them when they ran short.

Evan loved his family. He enjoyed being with them, talking to his brothers about nothing much at all. And the open fields that he could roam alone or with them. But he needed to be away too, having his own space and his own things. If he did quit his job and came home, his mom and dad would expect him to live with them again, as most of his brothers were. Not that it wasn't nice being all together, but he needed quiet sometimes.

Grandpa was at the house when they came out of the barn. He was still looking lost, not that Evan didn't blame him. Evan saw a lot of death in his job. Being a surgeon was not meeting people in the best of circumstances. His family might drive him nuts at times, but they were his and he loved them.

Hugging Grandpa, he followed him to the mudroom to clean up. Grandpa didn't say anything, but Evan knew he had something on his mind.

9

"You still a doctor out there in the city?" He said that he was. "I was wondering if you'd do me a favor when you go back. I need something notarized, and I'd like for you to drop me at the bank when you leave here. If you don't mind."

"Sure, but I know a couple of people that can do that, Mom for one. I think she still has her license up to date." He said he wanted the banker to do it. "I can take you. But if you don't mind, what is it?"

"I want to turn over my house to your daddy." Evan was drying his hands when he asked him why. "I just don't think I can live there anymore. It's got all them memories and it hurts me."

"Where are you going to live if not there?" He looked away. "Grandpa, if you don't tell me I'm going to start guessing, and I don't think I like that any better than you not telling me the truth."

"I can't go on. I just don't have it in me anymore to want to. I miss her that much." It hurt Evan to hear him say that. "I loved her for over sixty years, and now she's gone. What's a man supposed to do if he can't have the one love of his life standing beside him?" Evan hugged him again. "Oh, Evan, she was my entire world, she was. And the best thing that ever happened to me."

"Dad thinks you're going to end your life. Is that the plan? Because I have to tell you, I'm not going to let you. None of us will." Grandpa told him that he didn't have anything to live for. "You have us. Dad and Mom too. We'd have no one if you were to do this."

"I hurt." Evan told him he didn't know the pain he was feeling, but understood. "She kept me in line. Helped me through the day just by loving me. And I tell you right now that she made me feel like I was the king of the world with just her smile. I miss her so very much."

He sobbed then, holding onto Evan as he did so. Evan felt his own eyes fill with tears, and when they fell over his cheeks, he held his grandpa all the tighter. Grandma had been there for all of them. She'd been the one that he could go to for anything. And now she was gone and Grandpa wanted to join her.

Dinner was a somber affair. No one, it seemed, was in their usual jolly mood. Even Blake, who could liven up any seating, was quiet. Evan helped his mom clear the dishes, and the rest of them cleaned up the kitchen. Grandpa joined them just as they were putting the last clean pot on the hanger.

"Buy it from me. One of you boys, you should buy my house from me." They didn't move, not even to look at one another. "I will make you a good deal. I can't.... I was thinking of moving in with Oliver here, and I would love for one of you yahoos to have the house."

"You move in with Dad and Mom, and I'll buy it." Evan had no idea why he said that. He didn't need a house any more than he needed to work. "You promise us that you'll move in here and behave yourself, then I'll buy your house."

"I don't want to behave myself. I want to...I want to run in the woods. Have some.... You six should make me a great grandpa. I'd surely have something to do if you were to do that." Each of them groaned and Grandpa laughed. "You promise me that you'll be on the outlook for yourself a mate, and I'll try and keep myself in a better frame of mind."

"Deal." All of them put out their hands after making the promise. If that was all it took, a promise, then Evan would do

11

it. As for the house? He didn't have a clue what he was going to do with it, but he'd figure out something. Maybe he'd let his brothers use it for a while.

~~~

Norris put the phone in the cradle and looked at his dad. "She's coming home. They've made arrangements to pick her up and take her to the hospital in New York so that they can evaluate her before she can come here. It'll be about three more days or so before they release her to the one here in town. We'll have her close enough that we can go and visit her when we want to."

"Who?" Norris told him that Dylan was coming home. "Your momma is already here, Norris. You go on talking like she isn't, I'm going to have to ground you. I told you that before."

"Yes, Dad." Norris sat there, not mentioning to his dad again that his mom had died several years ago, and that he'd been living with them for seven years. Nor did he explain, again, that Dylan was his daughter, his dad's granddaughter, and that she was coming home because she'd been hurt badly and had to leave the service. He could tell him, but Dad wouldn't remember it.

"I'd like to have fish for dinner tonight. You go ask your momma if she can whip me some up." Norris nodded. "Then we should go for ice cream. You got those good grades, so we should celebrate. Didn't you, boy?"

"I'd like that. We'll go after supper, if you still want." Dad got up and made his way to his room. In a few minutes, he'd come back out and ask Norris where his bed was, and he'd have to show him. Alzheimer's sucked.

12

Several years ago his dad had been a little forgetful. Slightly disoriented at times too. Nothing that worried them much. His dad was brilliant, and had always had trouble remembering simple tasks unless he wrote them down. After his wife passed, he became worse…his inability to remember to put on shoes or wear a coat had gotten him put in the hospital with a cold that had turned into pneumonia. Then they started noticing his forgetfulness of who they were, and most of the time he would remember things that were well in the past.

Then he'd begun to wander off. It was then that Norris had found out that his dad was slowly losing his ability to do a great many things. Like living alone and keeping his own house. Meals were skipped because he couldn't remember if he'd eaten. Bedtimes were overlooked because he didn't recall where his bed was. Things like that and more had gotten the doctor to declare him unfit to live on his own. He'd been living with them since then.

Not that he didn't enjoy having his dad around. But lately, just over the last few months, he'd been getting away from them. Running off without telling anyone where he was going. And sometimes the police had to help them find him. His dad was having more and more bad days all the time. It was putting a strain not just on Norris's health, but his finances as well.

When Norris's wife, Stella, returned from grocery shopping, he checked on his dad before he went to help bring things in and saw that he was napping. They used to do all kinds of things together before his dad came to stay, now they had to do things in stages. But he was glad that he had his dad and that he could be there for him. He told Stella about the phone call he'd gotten.

"Dylan will spend a few weeks in the hospital here, then

they'll let her come home. I don't think she's going to be too terribly happy about that." Stella said that she could bet on that. "I'm so worried about her. We were lucky, they told me again. I'd have been a lot happier if she'd not gone over there at all."

"You couldn't have stopped her. She has her own mind, and once she gets something in it, she's not going to stop. Not even when it's that dangerous." Norris nodded. "To have her home will be wonderful. I know that she's going to need a lot of rehabilitation, but I'm so glad that she's coming home for good."

Dylan, Hutch to her men and friends, had been hurt badly about six months back. She and her men had been on a mission, something that she did a great deal while in the army, and she'd gotten hurt. Three of her men had been killed, and another had died right after he'd gotten to the hospital. Dylan nearly had too. Norris didn't know where it had happened or how she'd been injured, nor did he know to what extent her injuries were. But he knew that she was lucky to be alive, and that was all that mattered to him. For now, anyway.

"When did they say they'd be here with her? You probably told me, but my mind is a little fuzzy. I'm so tired, Norris. I shouldn't have stayed up so late watching that movie." He laughed and told his wife that it was supposed to be Friday. "Good. We'll be there when they land. Then we'll go to the hospital with her. I miss her so much."

He did as well, and had for a long time. Dylan was their only child, and she'd been a delightful little girl who grew up into a wonderful woman. At seventeen, she'd joined the army, and soon after she made it through boot camp, she'd been picked to be trained for special jobs. He knew that she

14

was covert, but anything else had been kept from them, to keep them, and especially her, safe.

Over the next ten years they'd seen very little of their daughter. She was forever rushing off for one thing or another, her job keeping her away for longer periods of time. Then about six months ago, a few days before they'd been notified that there had been an accident, she'd called him. With it coming in the middle of the night, he knew something was wrong.

"Dad?" He said it was him and glanced at the clock. He'd never forget the time. It was one twenty-four in the morning. "Dad, I'm going to be coming home soon, I've arranged it and I'll have a month off. I'd like for you to do something for me."

"Anything. You name it and it'll be yours." She laughed and he could hear the tension in it. "What is it, baby? Are you all right?"

"No. I've been...I don't think I can do this anymore. So much death and pain here now." He asked her what it was. "I can't tell you. But I'm done. I want to come home and make a life. After my R&R, I'm going to muster out. I want a house, a yard of my own. I want things to be normal."

"Normal? Honey, do you even know what that means?" She laughed again, and he could hear the little hiccup of a sob then. "Dylan, what is it? Tell me. I want to help you."

"There's this house, about two doors down from yours and Mom's. Buy it for me. I have the money. I'm sending you money that I have here to the account that you set up for me, and that we now use for Grandda." He heard her tell someone to fuck off and started to ask her what was going on, but she started talking again. "If you can, get it cheaper so I can have it retrofitted for Grandda. I want him to live with me."

"Honey, he's a lot to take on. Even for the two of us." It tore at his heart when she again told him she wanted to come home and have a normal life. "Dylan, what is going on?"

"I can't tell you. I can't...I'll come home for good, then we can talk. All right?" He said that he would look forward to it. "Buy the house. Like I said, the money is in the account that you opened for me when I was a little girl. I want you to use it to buy the house. The rest of it...you do with whatever you need to do to get you and Mom something nice."

He told her he would buy the house and she said she had to go. The line went dead then, and it had been the last time he'd spoken to her. Not even when they'd gone to see her was she able to speak. Her body was too broken to do much more than just heal. Norris made his way out to the back of the house and sat on the deck. His baby was coming home, and he doubted very much anything was going to be normal for her again.

"Norris?" He looked up at his wife when she said his name. "Norris, I can't find your father. He was resting not ten minutes ago, and now he's gone."

His body tensed up and he stood. Dad could have gone anywhere in that little time. The man was like a magician when it came to escaping their notice and getting into trouble. After calling the police to tell them what had happened, he began walking the streets. His dad would only be able to tell someone where he lived if he was having a good day. And his dad's good days had been few and far between in the last several weeks. Most everyone knew him, but there were a few that didn't.

"Did you find your dad, Mr. Hutchinson?" He told the officer that he'd not about an hour later when he drove up behind him. "I have all our men out looking for him. You should go and talk to Mr. Whitfield like I suggested. Him and his boys, they'd sure be able to find him a good deal faster."

"I know. I've been meaning to, but my daughter...she's coming home soon." Officer Petty told him that was wonderful as he stopped the cruiser and got out. "She's going to be spending a few weeks in the hospital, but she'll be home soon enough."

"You've had a rough few months, Mr. Hutchinson. But having Hutch home, that'll take some of the burden off you and your family. She was always one to depend on." He only nodded, knowing that she'd be depending on them a great deal now. He'd not been able to tell anyone anything because, frankly, he didn't know anything. "I've got my men out looking for him, sir, like I said. We'll find him for you."

He hoped so. While it wasn't cold out, as it was still summer yet, he did worry about his dad taking a tumble into something and not getting out. Or wandering into someone's home. He'd done that before as well. Norris walked the streets while calling out his name, hoping to find him soon.

Norris was exhausted when they finally found him three streets over and lost. Not just exhausted from looking for his dad, but that was a part of it. He was just tired of all the adulting he'd had to do of late. Smiling, he thought of what Dylan would say to him if he whined to her about it. She'd tell him to buck up and to fucking let it go. She had gotten a mouth on her since she'd gone away. And while it did embarrass him at times, he thought it was funny when she'd get on a roll with it. Like the time she'd come home for Christmas about five years ago.

"I have to go into town and pick up your mother's gift. Want to hang out with your old man?" She nodded and grinned at

17

him. "Please promise me that we're not going to get arrested. You will behave yourself, won't you?"

"Ah, Pop, why would I do that? I'm here to have fun." He groaned and she'd laughed at him. "Besides, what sort of trouble can I get into at the mall? I mean, they still have those mall cops running around, don't they?"

"Yes. And Bennie is still one of them. I swear to you, if you make him wet his pants again, I'll...I'll...." She laughed hard at his lack of a threat. "He's a good kid, Dylan. Why do you dislike him so much?"

"He's not a good kid, Dad. He's a bully and a fucking prick. But I'll be good if he does. Now, what did you get Mom?" By the time they'd gotten to the mall, both had been having a good time. When they went into the jeweler's, she'd offered to pay the difference on the watch he'd gotten for her mom.

"I got it. What did you get her?" She only shook her head and told him not to guess. "You did get her something, didn't you?"

"I got you both something." Norris had seen her stiffen up and turned to see Bennie behind him. "Hello, Bennie."

"Well, well, well. If it's not the terror of Washington street. Home for good, this time, Dylan? Or are you headed back to out of country?" Bennie made those quotation signs with his fingers when he asked her the last part. "Me and the boys, we think you're just in prison. A girl like you, that's where you belong."

"Dad?" He hadn't wanted trouble, not then or now, but there really was something simply mean about Bennie today. And after that, he'd noticed it a great deal more. "Dad, I'm doing what you asked, but it's not easy."

"You shoplifting, Dylan? Is that what you learned in prison? Or, I'm sorry, in the Army?"

Bennie reached for her, and even standing there beside her, Norris hadn't seen her move. Before he could tell her to go for it, Bennie was on the floor screaming to be released.

"You fucking broke my hand." She laughed and told him she'd not. "You have. I can feel it."

"No, I didn't. I only stopped you from touching me. However, I can break it if you want." Norris told her not to just yet. "All right. But I did try to be good, Dad. He started it."

"He did. I saw it."

The police were called and she was asked to let the mall cop go. After several witnesses said that she'd not done anything but defend herself, she was released. Norris had heard a few days later that not only had Bennie lost his job, but other women had come forward about his behavior in the mall. Bennie hadn't faired all that well after that.

Norris made his way out to the driveway to get his car. Stella had forgotten to get fish, and since Dad would eat if he had something he requested, they accommodated him when they could. Climbing into his car, he vowed that as soon as he was home again he was going to make a call to the Whitfields. Norris knew that they were tigers, but not much more than that. They were from money and didn't travel the same circles as he and his family did.

CHAPTER 2

Evan was home for the weekend again when he saw the man standing by the tree. He was careful not to scare him. The man was talking, but Evan wasn't sure if he was talking to himself or if someone was with him. As his cat, Evan wasn't taking any chances of getting himself hurt.

They were on private property, and that was grounds for being arrested if it came to that. Hunters had been warned before about his parents' land, but he didn't want to get shot over it. When the man turned and looked at him, Evan calmed his cat. He didn't want him chasing him if he ran.

"Hello, kitty." The man sounded happy to see him, which was odd. He was a big tiger, not a kitten. "Can I pet you? Oh, my son would love to have a picture with you. I'm betting that he's not going to believe his old man when I tell him I saw a pretty cat."

Moving closer, careful of the elderly man and who might be with him, Evan saw that he was shoeless and that his shirt was torn. Once he was close enough for the man to touch him, Evan could smell the drugs. He was ill, very much so.

"Come on now, have a little seat with me." He laid down

21

and the man leaned against him when he sat as well. He was quiet then, not moving but looking around the forest. Evan called to his dad to let him know what he'd found.

Older man? Gray hair and a pair of dark pants on? He told him that was right. *His name is Bailey Hutchinson. His family has been looking for him for a couple of hours. I'll let them know that you have him. Evan, he's got Alzheimer's, so go easy with him.*

I will, Dad. We're out by the creek at the back of the property. He's just sitting with me. Calling me a kitten. Dad laughed. *I'll stay with him until someone comes.*

"I'm having a good day today." The man turned and looked at him, and Evan could see that he was in a different frame of mind than he had been. "I'm not sure how I got here. Or where I am. I'm thinking you're not just a tiger either."

He shook his head at the man, who leaned down to lay his head on Evan's back. They sat there for a few more minutes until the man started crying.

"I'm a burden to my son and his wife. Just an old man who can't even remember what his name is half the time. My wife, she used to take care that I didn't embarrass myself or her, but she's gone now. I'm living with my son, Norris Hutchinson, and his wife, Stella." Evan wished that he could talk to him, but in order to do that, he'd have to shift and be naked. He knew that would scare Mr. Hutchinson, and he didn't want him hurt. "My son is a good man, he's been caring for me for a few years now, but I'm thinking I need more than he's able to give me."

Evan could hear someone coming, and tensed a little until he saw his dad and grandda coming through the woods. They were both men, which Evan was grateful for, and they started talking to Mr. Hutchinson as they made their way to them.

22

"Hello, Bailey. I heard you were around. Found yourself a cat there, didn't you?" Mr. Hutchinson said that he did, as a matter of fact. "That there is my grandson, Evan. I bet you remember him."

"Your grandson? No, can't say that.... Is he the one that's the surgeon at the medical hospital?" Dad told him he was. "Well, I'll be dogged. I haven't seen him in years. A surgeon, is he? Well that's just grand."

Evan told his dad what the man had told him before they had arrived. *It's sad the way that disease takes the best part of a person. Memories are something that I hold dear to me. You go on now and let us walk him back to the house. His son is on his way out.*

"No, please don't leave me." Evan stilled when the elderly man wrapped his hand in his fur when he started to leave. "Please, just don't leave me. I don't know where I am."

His mind had slipped again, Evan knew. There was a panicked look in his eyes. His fingers were tight in his fur, not painfully, but close enough. He waited to see if he'd come back to himself, but it appeared that his moment of clarity was gone for now.

He stayed with him. They all walked back to the house, Bailey with his hand in his fur and his dad and grandpa on either side of them. By the time they were clearing the trees, the man was sobbing about not knowing where he was again, and that he missed his little boy. Evan watched the man and woman on the porch to see if they'd be mad at their father for scaring them. Evan stayed with him as his cat to keep the elderly man calm.

The man, Norris Hutchinson, looked so relieved to see his dad that he felt bad for him. Evan had worked in the hospital long enough to know what sort of problems could arise with a man as far gone in his disease as Bailey was.

"Dad? Did you have a nice visit? Next time you go out, you'll have to let us know. We might have wanted to go with you." Bailey asked who the man was. "I'm Norris, Dad. This is Stella, my wife. Dylan is coming home soon."

"Norris? I thought you were a little boy." He assured him that he was all grown up. "I was out looking for cats for you. I know that you love kittens."

"Thanks, Dad. That's really sweet of you." Norris looked at him, and Evan felt sorry for him. "I need to ask you a favor, please. I should have done it before, and please don't feel obligated to say yes. The police suggested that I contact you so that you could find him easier."

"I'm not lost, Norris. I'm right here." Bailey looked at him. "Well, look at that. A kitty. My son, he loves kittens. I'm thinking of getting him one."

Dad, ask Mr. Hutchinson to dinner, please? I'd like to help him out. Next time he might not be so lucky at one of us happening upon him.

Evan went into the house to change. His clothing was packed to go back to town, but this was important. When he shifted and dressed, he thought of the man. To even think you were a burden would be hard on anyone. He was also going to talk to the family. Tell them what Bailey had said to him.

Dinner was ready by the time he made his way down the stairs. Last weekend when he'd been home, he'd made a deal with his grandpa. Now he owned a house that he wasn't sure that he'd ever stay in, and his grandpa was living with his mom and dad. So far it seemed that it was working out. But then it had only been a week. He sat down at the table with Norris and told him he'd help.

"I don't know what it might involve. I can't...we've lost him before, you see, but never for this long. Last weekend he made his way to a couple of streets over. Today.... Well, today you found him. It's getting harder and harder to keep him safe." Evan nodded and passed him the potatoes. "He has moderate to severe Alzheimer's. He has good days, but not as many as he used to have. And my daughter, she's in the hospital here in town now, and we can't take him with us when we visit her. He doesn't like hospitals, and they make him upset. So only one of us can go and see her at a time, and it's very tiring on the other of us to be left alone with Dad. Not that we don't love him to pieces, but like I said, he's a handful."

"Do you have outside help with him? Someone to come in and take over for a little while so that you and your wife can be alone?" He said that he had tried, but it was hard to find someone that could do it even for a little bit, and it was expensive as well. "I understand. I know a few nurses that are retired that can help you out. And, as you said, if it's money, I'm sure that you can work something out with them about that as well."

"I don't want him to feel like we've abandoned him. He's all I have left now." Evan said he could understand that as well. He'd just lost his grandma. "Today, when he got away, we had someone keeping an eye on him. No one does as good as job as my wife and I, it seems. But we thought for just an hour he'd be all right. I guess we were wrong about that too."

"No, you weren't wrong. But finding the right person for the job can be hard. I had a patient once whose wife was ill with the same thing. He finally had to have help at home when he was operated on. It was just a person from their church who had little to no understanding of the illness, and he didn't get the rest that he needed. It became so much for him that he ended up joining her in a nursing home a few weeks later. You need help, Mr. Hutchinson. You will wear yourself down if you don't get it." He nodded and looked so sad. "I know that you love your father, sir, I'm not saying that you don't. But he's not going to get any better."

"No, we know that as well. And to be honest with you, I don't have any idea what we're going to do when Dylan gets out of the hospital. She's going to need as much, if not more care, than my dad does. I don't know the real extent of her injuries, no one would tell us, but it was bad. She nearly died." Evan would look into her when he got back to work tomorrow. In the meantime, he was going to help this man. "I have to have help. I know that now. If you could give me the names of those nurses, I'll contact them too."

After dinner, he sat down with the couple and his family. Dad explained that they'd need to have only a taste of his skin and his scent and they'd be able to find him, so long as he never got into a car when he was gone. They also talked about taking their blood as well, just to be safe.

"Yes, I can understand that. All right." Norris looked at his dad and told him what was going to happen. Bailey didn't understand, that much was clear, but he allowed each of them to lick his skin and sniff at his neck. Then they did so to the son and his wife.

"You'll be able to find him now? As your cats?" Dad told him they could find him either way, but the cat was easier. "I don't know how to thank you for this. Not just for finding him today, but for everything. It's been so long.... Well, it's been too long since we've asked for help. I'm so glad that you're not turning us down."

By the time the Hutchinsons left, Evan had a list of things he was going to do for them. First, he was going to find them help, and secondly, find out about the daughter. Maybe she was having something done that was unnecessary...things like that really pissed him off. Then she was going to sponge off her parents until she was well enough to face the world again. Evan had a lot of things to do in the morning.

He had no idea why he thought that about their daughter. Of late he'd been having ill thoughts regarding just about anyone. Evan thought it was his job, or perhaps he just needed a long vacation. Whatever it was, he needed to be a lot calmer or he was going to be in trouble. Evan tried his best to calm himself before he drove back to the city.

~~~

Hutch was trying her best not to lose her temper again. But if one more person told her how lucky she was to be alive and that she needed to be more cooperative, she was going to pull out her gun and shoot them all. She looked over the head of the nurse who was taking her blood pressure when her commanding officer walked in.

"Not in the best of humor, are you, Hutch?" Randy Delaney sat in the room's only chair and smiled at her. "Someone said that you were already biting heads off this morning, and pissing in people's oats. Didn't I ever tell you that you make more friends with honey than you do—?"

"I don't give a good fuck about having friends. This fucking shit hurts." He laughed and the nurse left her. She'd not even taken the stupid machine that she'd been using with her. "When the hell can I get out of here? You said a few days. It's been a fucking week."

"I said a few weeks, not days. And you can't leave until they say you're fit. Which might be longer than you think if you keep getting your panties all bunched up. Calmness is what you need, not making everyone here scared to death of you." She told him that she liked them being afraid of her. "Won't work on me, Hutch. I know that deep down you're a softy. You should let a little more of that out when you have to deal with people."

"I don't like people. They want things from me." He asked her what. "Never mind. I just want to know what you're doing about getting me back to work."

They'd talked a great deal since she'd been home. Well, not home, but in this stupid hospital. Randy had been nothing but honest with her, telling her that she wasn't going to be able to do her job any longer. That being hurt the way she was and how it had happened was the end. She didn't want it to end. Hutch wanted to go back where rules were enforced and she wasn't told to be nice.

"I told you before, you're done." Hutch looked away. She didn't want to be done now. Before, yes. It had been a shitty couple of days, but now she knew that she needed this job to help her mom and dad out. "I do have some information on the combat that you were in. There wasn't much left in the way of evidence when we finally got there, but just enough that we know that you and your men were lucky to have gotten out."

"Some of my men were not so lucky." He told her he was

sorry. "What happened? It was supposed to be a simple get in and get out mission. You said yourself that no one would be hurt. Now I have four dead men, a couple of dozen dead civilians, as well as enough damage to have warranted a full out evac of the rest of the people. Where did we go wrong?"

"Don't know. As I told you before, I'm looking." He was hiding something from her, but she was in too much pain to quibble with him. "You taking your shit? They said you could have something every four if you want it."

"I don't. I don't want to be doped up when my parents come by." He asked her if she thought them seeing her in pain was better. "I don't think they're noticing that. They're thrilled to have me back again."

"Maybe if you keep snapping at them like you do other people, they'll wish you gone again. You know, a few months ago you were telling me that you were done. Now you're wanting back in. What the fuck happened in the last few days?" Hutch said nothing, but did look at her legs. "Dylan, tell me what changed your mind."

When Randy called her by her first name, she knew he was being serious. Her mom called her Dylan Stella when she was in trouble. But Randy used her first name. She looked up at him, then away again before answering him.

"I have a house here. My dad bought it for me just before I got hurt. It was supposed to be for my grandda and me. Now I can't even care for myself, much less him too. I need to go back so that someone can whip me back into shape." He only stared at her. "It's about the money, if you want to know the truth. I need the money and the insurance. I can't be burdening my parents any more than they already are. I had no idea my grandda was so bad."

It was mostly a lie, but he didn't seem to know it. And if he did, he'd not call her on this one. It was all true to a point. She did want to get into shape again. She did own a house, but getting back into the service would get her killed. That's what she was hoping for. Her parents could do a lot with the kind of money that her insurance was worth. Hutch wanted them to be set up for life, even if hers was over now.

"I'm useless to them, you know that. I can't walk without some major pain right now. And, according to the doc here, I might never be able to have children. Not really a big deal since I can't stand people, but that's just a thing on my list. My insides are all fucked to hell too. I can't get a job, not with things like they are in this town." He nodded as if he understood what she was saying. "I want to reenlist so that I can have something to fill my days. A way to make some money so that I can send it to my parents. That's not too much to ask for, is it?"

"No. But it's not going to happen. They're not going to allow you to do that, Hutch. I've explained that to you. You're a hero to them, someone that they want to cherish until you push up daisies. And while we're on that subject, you're not going to go back because I won't have you stepping in front of an IED and ending your life." Hutch looked at him. "Yes, I know you're thinking of what sort of shit you can get into if I were to allow you to return. An Improvised Explosive Device would take care of your pain permanently, but it would also hurt everyone that you knew. Including your parents."

There wasn't anything to say to him that would change his mind. Instead of wasting her breath arguing with him, she decided that she'd do what she wanted some other way. Hutch wasn't going to be a burden on her family. They had enough to deal with because of Grandda.

"You do have options, you know. I could put you on a desk. Recruit for us." She told him no fucking way. "Or I can put you on some dock somewhere, and you could teach sailors how to curse. I'm pretty sure they could learn a thing or two from you."

Before she could tell him what she thought of that, her doctor came in the room. He had someone with him, but that didn't bother her. This was a teaching hospital, and they'd been coming in and out of her room since she'd been here. When the man moved, she saw the gun and looked at Randy. He nodded once and stood up. There was something shitty going on, she thought.

"Hello, Sergeant Hutchinson. I've come to.... I've been...."

The man behind the doctor shoved him out of the way. He drew his gun at the same time that she did hers. Randy had his gun pointed at the door so that no one else could come in. The doctor wasn't moving, so she ignored him for the moment.

"You're Hutchinson?" Hutch nodded but didn't lower her gun when he told her to. "You're supposed to be dead."

"Yeah, I get that a lot. What the fuck are you doing in here, other than getting your ass killed?" He laughed. "You think I'm comical? My CO doesn't. He thinks I have a potty mouth and a bad attitude. I can't really fault him for that, but it's you we're talking about now. What are you doing in my room?"

"I've come to kill you. My son is dead because of you and yet here you are, living it up while he's cold in his grave. He was my world and you took him from me. How could you do that? He was just a boy." She didn't bother looking at Randy

31

when he moved. "It's not fair. Not fair at all that you're alive and my boy isn't. You have to die too."

The man looked at the doctor, then back at her. She knew what he was going to do when he started to lower the gun to the man on the floor. He was going to kill the doc to get her to cooperate. No fucking way would another death be on her head.

"You take your aim off of me for a split second and you're dead. I'm sure you know that." The door opened behind them both and the man turned. When he did she fired, hitting him in the shoulder, and his gun went flying. The man wouldn't die but he wouldn't shoot anyone either. Not today anyway.

He was falling to the floor when Randy had the other man pinned to the floor with a gun at the back of his head. The room was suddenly filled with people. Mostly staff, but she put her gun down when told to and put her hands over her head. The man on the floor who Randy was holding, a doctor she thought, hadn't moved either when Randy started barking orders to call the police. Hutch was hurting so bad that had she been able to move, she was sure she'd pass out.

"The police are on their way." Hutch nodded as Randy stood up. "Hutch? Are you all right? Did he hit you?"

"I don't think so. But I fucking hurt." The man on the floor laughed. "How about you stand him up and let me shoot at him too? I'm sure that'll take the funny right out of his day."

"Please don't. My mom is going to be pissed enough that I was in on this. She hates when her boys get hurt." The doctor was helped up by Randy. When he was told not to move, he stared at her while Randy patted him down. "You're Norris Hutchinson's daughter?"

"Yes. How do you know my dad?" He told her that he'd found her grandda over the weekend when he got lost. "Thank you, but that doesn't explain why you're in my room. I have enough shit going on without having some white jacket prick coming in to order more tests."

"You're not very friendly, are you?" She just smiled at him, and picked her gun up and pointed at him. "I came in here to find out a little more about you. I had it all wrong, I can tell that now. But what did that man mean by you getting his son killed and he was going to return the favor? I mean, I can guess if he's spent much time with you, but I'd like to know."

"Wow, nice bedside you got there, dickweed. You might want to curb that before someone takes you to task." The banter was fun but she was hurting too bad for it to go on. She laid her head back and closed her eyes for a moment to let some of it mellow out. "I don't know who you are, nor do I give a fuck, but if you could get me something for pain, I'd really appreciate it."

She heard him move then talk to someone in the hall. Looking beneath her lashes, she could see that the police had arrived and she took her hand off the weapon. They'd take it from her now, but Randy would give her another one so she didn't let it bother her too much. She wasn't sure what was going on, but she was going to get to the bottom of it before someone returned to finish the job.

"Hutch, they need for you to give up your weapon." Nodding at Randy made her sicker. She'd moved her hand away from it but they wouldn't take it without her permission. She was still too close for them to be comfortable. But there wasn't any fucking way she was going to move again without hurting someone. "I'm going to take it from you, all right?"

"Hurt. Yes, take it, but I fucking hurt. Randy, you have to get me something for the pain." He told her he knew, she was bleeding. "I think I broke something in me. I have a better idea…just let me go and I'll bleed out."

Someone said something like not today, but she wasn't sure who that was. The drugs were kicking in now. Hutch wasn't even aware that anyone had given her any until then. As she began to feel less and less like she had been run over, she opened her eyes and looked at the doc again.

"You gave me the good stuff." He said he had, and for her to let it work. "Why don't you just pull the plug, Doc? It'll be a huge favor to me if I can just keel over right now."

"I don't think so. So long as I'm alive you're not going to die." That was strange, but she was too loopy to figure it out. "Let it take you under, Dylan, and when you wake, we'll talk about this mouth of yours."

"My mouth is just fine." But it wasn't. She was having a hard time making it work. "That man, I should have let him shoot me."

"Not today." That was the last thing she heard before the drugs took her under.

CHAPTER 3

Evan made his rounds, but kept thinking about the woman. He'd only gone into her room to find out what sort of shit she was pulling when he'd been caught right up in her life. Her CO, Randy Delaney, had taken him aside and explained why there wasn't a true accounting of her injuries on the file that he'd looked at.

"There are any number of factions that would come for her. As you noticed today, some people, their families, are none too happy with what happened over there. More precisely, what they don't know happened. Some of her squad was killed, and since we can't tell them the true reason, they'll take it out on her." Evan asked why. "A great many reasons, none of which, as I said, I can share with you. But we thought she'd be safe, at least for the time being until we could get her out of here. Apparently, someone knows that she's getting better now."

"Mr. Bean, he said his son was killed. What is it you told him that would send him here?" Randy said nothing, and he had a feeling that he wasn't going to. "She's in my hospital, Mr. Delaney, with patients that I care for. How much more of this can we expect?"

"I'm hoping none, but with people, you can't ever tell. But I have put on more security for her. And I've given her a gun." Evan told him he didn't want her to have it. "I understand that. But let me ask you something, Doctor Whitfield. When you get here, to work, you put on that tie and lab coat. Correct?"

"My lab coat is not a gun. There is a huge difference." Delaney told him it wasn't for her. "I will hold you responsible if anyone gets killed because you gave her a gun."

"All right. But if she pulls her weapon and needs to use it, I guarantee you, it will be justified. She might even manage to save your ass if you need it. She's that fucking good." Evan nodded. There was very little that he could say or do to keep her from having a weapon, but Randy thanked him. "Also, Doctor, you might see a few new faces on this floor. I've set up nurses and other staff to be on the safe side."

She was good, he'd said. At what, Evan wanted to ask the man, but he'd walked away. And even after all this time, he really wasn't sure he wanted to know. She was good.... She was also his mate.

Evan had been trying for the last few hours to talk himself out of that thought. No matter how many times he tried to convince himself otherwise, his cat would tell him that he was a fool. Well, not tell him, but he did want to go back and make her his. Stretching his neck, he looked at the chart in his hands to try and remember what he was doing.

"Doc?" He smiled at Justin Rogers. "You've been standing there for five minutes. You okay? You looked wigged out. You got the flu, or you have to go to the bathroom?"

"Wigged out? Yes, that's about right. I feel that way too. How are you feeling today, Justin? Any more pain in that leg?"

He said that he was doing better at therapy too. "Good. And the next time you get a cut on your body anywhere, you have to tell your mom. It's important when you're a diabetic. I think we talked about that."

"We did, but it's the last weeks of summer and I didn't want to have to be all wrapped up when I could be out playing." Evan told him he'd not get to play much if they had to take his leg. "I know. Mom is sore at me for not telling her too, but I promised her that I'd be more careful."

"Good. And you're to watch your carbs too. I know that you're aware of what you can and can't eat. Stick to that, Justin, or this won't go well for you." He nodded and Evan sat down on the bed with him. "If you do well over the next few days, and promise to keep to the rules, I think I can let you go home Friday. That way you'll have a week before school starts to hang out with your buddies. Okay?"

"Yes. Thanks." He smiled and Evan returned it. "You need to talk about what's wigging you out. Is it a girl?"

"Might be. What do you do when you have a girlfriend that's not quite what you expected?" The young boy stared at him. "You know, sort of the opposite of what you are."

"Girls are weird, Doc. I mean, sheesh, they're all out there, I think. And if she's way opposite of you, then run away. That's what I do when Mary tells me to hold her hand." Evan asked him if he liked Mary. "No. Gosh, she's a girl. Nobody should like girls. They're weird, like I said."

Evan smiled. When you asked an eight-year-old about women troubles, then you'd get an eight-year old's answer. Ruffling up Justin's hair, he stood up and told him he'd see him tomorrow. The kid had a heart of gold, it seemed, but the illness of someone older.

He found himself outside her room again an hour later. The officer there checked his identification, called into someone on his phone to verify it, and then patted him down before he could go inside the room. Evan was glad they were watching over her like this, and wondered what she'd have when she left here. He went into her room after a brisk knock, even though she'd not bid him entry.

"You're not my doctor…you know that, right?" He nodded at her and sat on the chair by her bed. "Well then, go away. I'm not in the mood to be social."

"I doubt very much if you're ever in the mood to be social. My name is Evan Whitfield, by the way." She didn't say anything. "As for being your physician, I am as of yesterday afternoon. I talked to your doctor and he and I traded a patient. I think you might be more difficult to take care of than Mrs. Conrad, who just had a heart valve put in."

"So? I didn't ask you to be my doc. And to be frank with you, I don't care either." He smiled. Christ, she was full of temper. "If you're not in here to release me, then I'd very much like it if you were to go away. I have enough shit to deal with because of the drugs they keep giving me."

"What kind of issues are you having with the drugs?" He stepped into the hall to get her chart brought to him. When he had it in his hand, he sat back in the chair. "It says here that you're not taking anything for pain. Why?"

"I don't like feeling loopy. Nor do I want to be drugged up if someone comes to visit me. I might have to be on my toes for that again." He nodded and looked at the rest of her information. "It's not the right chart…you know that, don't you?"

"No. Where is it if this isn't the right one?" She nodded to the wall where the closets were. He retrieved the file from the bottom of the locker-like cabinet and sat again. He was nearly to page four when he looked up at her. "Is this true?"

"Yes." She turned her head from him and looked out the window. "I can't tell you what went down, but my injuries on that are true. Broken femur, six ribs on the left, four on the right. Seventy-six stitches in my back. Second degree burns on my back and leg. I was shot numerous times in the abdomen as well as the chest. My jacket saved me from one or two to the heart. I have damage — their words, not mine — to my abdomen that has essentially taken away my ability to ever have a kid. Not that I want any, but I've been hurt enough that it would be a miracle to get knocked up." She looked at him then. "Of course, that could be a good thing. I could have numerous sexual partners and not have to worry who the baby daddy might be."

The growl startled them both. He found himself standing over her bed and leaning over her. She had beautiful blue eyes, freckles over the bridge of her nose, and full sexy lips. Licking his own, Evan found that he wanted to taste her in the worst kind of way.

"You're too close." He nodded, but didn't move. "You're not human, are you? I saw him. You're...I think you're a feline."

"Tiger. You know that much, then I'm sure you know about mates and how we are." She nodded and his cat snarled at him. When she moved back from him, as far as she could and still be on the bed, he saw her pain. "I won't hurt you. Not ever."

He started to lower his head when he felt it. The gun that he'd forgotten about was at his chest, pointed directly at his heart. Instead of backing from her, he moved his hand up her arm to the gun and held it there.

"I'll kill you." He thought of telling her that she wouldn't be able to hurt him, but with this woman, he wasn't so sure. "Back off and you'll live another day."

He kissed her. A quick touch of his mouth to hers before he moved back. Evan sat down…it was about all he could manage without any blood in his head. When he looked at her, he could see what it was costing her to hold the gun still pointed at him.

"I won't touch you again right now." She still hadn't lowered the gun. "I'm sorry that I made you have to pull that on me, but I swear to you, I'd never harm you. Put it down and I'll stay right where I am. I can see what kind of pain you are in because of it. I'm truly sorry, Dylan."

"It's Hutch. And you will if you think to claim me. I don't have time for bullshit romance. Not to mention, I don't care for it either. I don't want to be shackled to you any more than I want to be in this hospital." Evan didn't much care for her description of their relationship, but he was willing to let it go for now. "What makes you think that I'm your mate anyway?"

"Your smell." She glared at him. "Not that you smell, but that you have a scent that calls to me. And as you pointed out, my cat knows you for what you are. He wants to mark you. I do as well. But for now, I'm content with just sitting here speaking with you."

He wasn't and neither was his cat. And Evan had a feeling Dylan knew it. When she didn't lower the gun, but seemed to get stronger with his words, he nearly asked her what was so funny when she shook her head at him.

"Yeah, marked up enough, thanks. But you will stay where

you are." He started to laugh but didn't. "You need to leave here. Now. I not only don't want to be your mate, but I'm a wanted woman, by some very determined people. Not that I blame them, but I'd just as soon no one got hurt, no matter how stupid their intentions are, when they come for me."

He saw it then, the telltale signs that she wasn't just in pain, but it was making it difficult for her to think, even to breathe. But he had to assure her that she was going to be safe. He had no idea what he would do to keep her that way, but he wasn't going to let her get hurt.

"They'll never get to you." He watched her face; the pain was there and more powerful with every passing moment. It was like it was a part of her skin. "Let me help you, Dylan. I can get you something for that. If you'll let me. You're not going to heal well when you're hurting so badly."

"I can't breathe." He could see that she was blue around the lips and stood up. "Christ, I can't breathe, I hurt so bad. Fuck, just kill me now." Then she fainted.

~~~

Norris watched his little girl. His dad was being unusually quiet right now, so he enjoyed this brief break. When he got up he thought he was going to have to run him down again, but he only pushed his chair to the bed and picked up Dylan's hand.

"She's so hurt." Norris told him that she was. "I remember her being such a wonderful child. Forever wanting me to read her stories from that fat book of hers."

Norris laughed. "Yes, no faerie tales or romance for her. It was war and guts all the way. We should have known then that she wasn't going to be a girly girl." Dad laughed too. "Remember that little boy down the street from us? Thomas something. He sure did have a crush on her when she was about ten. He nearly wet himself when she kicked his butt on the playground a week later because he pulled on her little hair ribbons."

"She's my girl." Norris nodded and thought that his dad was slipping away again. Then he kissed the back of her hand and looked at him. "She's my baby girl, and if I could trade places with her, I'd do it. I hurt too, Norris. So very much when I can't even remember my own name."

"I love you, Dad. So very much. And once she's better, she'll spend lots of time with you." He nodded and laid his head down on her hand. "Dad, the nurse that comes to see you, she's helping you, right?"

When he didn't answer him, Norris leaned back in his seat. His daughter was in a great deal of pain, but it was what her doctor had told him that worried him the most. She wanted to die. He didn't understand that any more than his father's illness.

When Dylan had left for the Army, he'd been afraid for her. Not terrified like he had been later in her career, but he didn't want her to be hurt. Then about six months after she'd finished her boot training, she'd come home for a short leave to tell them that she'd been accepted into this special program.

"I won't be home as much, and I won't ever be able to tell you where I am." He'd asked her if it was Special Forces. "I can't tell you. But I'll be making enough money that I can help you here."

"We don't need for you to take on this job just to help out here, Dylan. We're doing just fine the way we are." She told him that she wanted a house, to live near them and lend a hand. "You'll have it if you save your money. And the money that you send us now, it goes a long way in making things easier for us."

"I want to do this, Dad. I need to. It's what I've wanted all my life. To help you and Mom the way you helped me when I needed it." He didn't want her to do it, but in the end, he'd given in. "Thank you, Dad. I know this is hard for you, but I want to help you while making a living too."

Not that she needed his permission, but he gave it to her all the same. And now this had happened. His daughter was fighting for her life, even her sanity, because she'd taken on a job for the government that had gotten some of her friends killed.

"Dad?" Norris sat up, and noticed that his dad was still lying on Dylan's hand when Dylan spoke again, quietly. "Dad, how long have you been here?"

"Not long." He took her other hand in his and held it to his cheek. "Grandda wanted to come in and see you. I didn't want to tell him no, not when he usually hates coming to the hospital so much. But we have help now, thanks to your doctor friend. He's been sending over someone every day to keep up with him so your mom and I can have a small break."

"That's wonderful. Grandda looks good, don't you think?" He nodded. They both knew that he no longer seemed like the man he was even a year ago. "When am I going to get to leave here? Has anyone said? And he's not my friend. He's a pain in the ass."

"No one has said. I guess you've had some minor setbacks and they want to keep an eye on you. As for Evan being your friend, he's a nice man. You should give him a chance, honey." She nodded and closed her eyes again. "Dylan, please don't

43

leave me. I need you, baby."

"I'm not going to be able to go back to work. At anything, Dad. Not now. I can recruit for the Army, but not much more than that. They're putting me out to pasture." He wanted to tell her that was wonderful, but he only nodded. "It's all I know how to do. What will I do outside of this mess? I can't be one of those people that sits around on their ass all day with nothing to occupy my head. I needed this. What the hell am I going to do now?"

"Live a full life." She told him that was no longer possible. "Why not? You're still in one piece, aren't you?"

"Sort of." He didn't know what that meant, but before he could ask, she continued. "I don't know how to eat until I'm told to. I don't own any clothing that's not camo or black. I wear combat boots every day. I can shoot a rifle, disassemble it if necessary, and I can break a man's neck without much effort. These are not job qualifications that usually are on an application."

"No, I would think not. But you'll think of something. You have always been good at bouncing back." She nodded, but looked so sad. "I like your new doctor, by the way. He's been good to us. Is he taking good care of you?"

"He's an asshole." The door opened behind him, and he didn't have to look to see it was the asshole. The look on Dylan's face would have been comical but for the fact that she looked so murderous. "I thought I told you to go away and leave me alone."

"You say a lot of things I don't think you mean about me. Like being an asshole." She flushed. His daughter actually looked embarrassed. Norris turned to look at Evan and told him he was glad to see him. "As I am you. I've been hearing good things about your dad. He loves to take long walks, Nora said."

"Yes. I take him when I can, but.... Well, I sometimes need the walk myself." He looked at Dylan as he stood up. "I'm assuming that he wants to look you over. Your mom said she'd be in later today. I'll take Grandda home so he can rest."

Dad was harder to wake up and get going. He'd slipped away again and didn't know where or who he was. He looked at Dylan when she called to him, but he shied away from her touching him. He was going down the hall with him when his dad told him he was tired.

"Me too, Dad. How about we go home, I make you some lunch, and we both take a little snooze?" Bailey smiled and nodded. "Then when Stella gets home, we'll think about coming back to see Dylan. Would you like that?"

"Dylan? You mean your momma is in the hospital again? I can't stand her being sick." He assured him that she was his granddaughter and she was getting better. "You have a wife, son? I didn't know you'd gotten married. Why wasn't I invited to the wedding?"

"You were there, Dad. You gave Stella away because her own dad is gone." His dad nodded, but Norris knew he was still confused. "You want to walk home, or do you want me to call a taxi for us?"

"Oh, let's walk. I love to walk. There is a bakery on Tenth that I like to look in their picture windows." He didn't tell him that the place had been gone for decades. He'd more than likely forget about it before they were in the area anyway. "And then when we get there, I want to buy a loaf of rye bread. I so love fresh rye bread."

He did like rye bread. And Norris decided to pick up a loaf or two when he was in town next time. Dad talked about things both present and past like they were somehow the same. Norris enjoyed the conversation, and how Dad would bring him into each story line. They were nearly home when he turned and looked at him. Norris was almost afraid of what he'd say.

"You're a good son, Norris. You always have been." He thanked him. "No need for that. I love you. So very much, son. I don't know what I would have done these last years had you not taken care of me."

"Dad, you took care of me when I was a kid. Having you in my home and living with us, it's the greatest pleasure a man could have from his father." He nodded and moved ahead again.

They were nearly to the house when his dad started laughing. It took him several seconds to see the dog that was pulling at its leash to get to his dad. But the closer his dad got to the dog, the more it started to snap and try to bite him. Luckily, the man who held the dog seemed to understand that it wasn't going to be a friendly visit. He snapped at his dad to stop.

"I don't know what's gotten into him. He usually only acts this way around cats or other dogs, but not like this." The dog seemed to be rabid to get to his dad, and when he started to back away, the dog was angrier. "I'm having some trouble holding onto him, Mr. Hutchinson. I'm sorry, but he's pretty upset. Perhaps we can do this some other time?"

"Yes. Maybe he's just got a cold or is mad about something." The man nodded and pulled his dog in the opposite direction. It was tough for the man too...he was really straining to hold the animal. When he was in his fenced yard the dog seemed to calm some, but he and his dad decided to take the long way home. "Burt doesn't like me."

"I'm sure that's not it." But his dad was inconsolable. Before they were in their own yard, his dad was sobbing like a child, clinging to him and telling him that he loved the dog and wanted to only pet him. "We'll give him a couple of days then go see him again. Maybe you brushed against a cat somewhere and he doesn't like the scent, that's all."

"It could be the doctor." Norris had no idea that his dad knew the Whitfields were cats. He had seen Evan as one, but he hadn't realized that his dad knew that it was a shifter and not a kitten as he'd called him. "I'll have to tell him no more hugs. That's what it is, I'm thinking. It's that nice doctor."

His dad went to his room when they got in the house. Norris heard the television turn on and his dad's laughter. Dad was set for the night, it seemed. In the morning, he'd have a talk with him about the dog. So long as Evan was around, the dog wasn't going to care for him. He might even think about getting his dad his own puppy. That might make him less inclined to find others to pet.

CHAPTER 4

Hutch wasn't sure what the hell the doctor was doing sleeping in the chair in her room, but she watched him. He was a tall, good looking man…not at all what she would have expected in a doctor. Not that she had a lot of knowledge about doctors, other than they seemed to be assholes who ordered people around. When she stretched out, her ribs caused her some pain and she moaned. That was all it took to wake him. He only stared at her, which made her a little uncomfortable. And snappy.

"Don't you have a life? Somewhere to go that's not here?" He stood up and stretched, his arms well over his head and lifting his scrubs up so that she could see his belly. "What the hell are you doing here?"

"I had a bad night and I wanted to come in and have a nice sleep with you. And since I know you'd hurt me if I joined you in the bed, I decided to sleep, uncomfortably mind you, in that chair." Not even thinking about him in the bed with her, she asked him about his bad night. "I lost a patient. He died on the operating table."

"I'm sorry. Was he a friend?" He told her all his patients

49

were his friends. "I mean, did you have a friendship with him before you became his doctor?"

"Yes. He was a friend of my grandpa's. Grandma's too, but she passed on a few months ago. How are you feeling today? Well enough to give me a morning kiss?" She stared at him. "No? Oh well, a man can try. I do have some good news for you. If you work hard in PT today, I'll allow you to go home with me."

"I'm not going home with you." He laughed. "Seriously. I don't want you to get it in your head that we're going to be anything to one another. I have things to do. A life that I want to get back to. Even as shitty as it is, you're not going to be a part of it."

"I'm sure you do, and I'm glad for you. As for it being shitty, I'm sure we can work on that as well. We're mates, Dylan. And you can deny that all you want, but that's what we are to each other." He sat back down, but when he stood up again, she reached under the blanket for her gun. "Delaney is coming. I haven't told him yet about us."

"There is no us, you moron. When are you going to get that into your thick head? The one above your belt line." The door opened just as she was speaking, and Hutch felt her face heat up when Randy laughed. "Have you done what I asked you to do yet?"

"So cranky. Are you this way all the time in the morning? If so, then I would hate to wake up beside you."

Before she could tell him what she'd told the moronic doctor, Evan was lifting Randy up by his throat and a foot off the floor. Randy didn't struggle but stared at Evan. When she told Evan for the fourth time to put him down, she thought for sure she was going to have to shoot him. As soon as Randy was released, he dropped to the floor and stayed there, holding his neck and glaring at Evan.

"Christ, you could have said something. I had no idea." Evan nodded and turned to look at her. Randy looked at her as well as he apologized to her. "I'm sorry. I shouldn't have been so callous. I mean, I figured the two of you were hooked up, but I didn't think about what—"

"I am not, nor will I ever be, hooked up to this man. Or any man for that matter. I haven't the foggiest idea where you think that is coming from, but I'm not his fucking mate." Neither of them moved, but Evan smiled at her. She wanted to get up and punch him in the balls. The fucker was making her insane. "I want you both to get out of here. Now. I don't want to see either of you again. Ever."

"I did what you asked." That shut her up, and she questioned if there had been any trouble. "No. Not at all. You have to go to the bank sometime and sign the paperwork, but you should be able to sell the house for what you purchased it for."

"And the money, it's in my parents' account?" He nodded. "Thank you. I hated to do that, but I want them to be secure."

"What happened?" When she didn't answer Evan, he looked at Randy. "You should know that I just bought a house. It's huge too. It was my grandparents' home. We can live there if you'd—"

"There is no us. And yes, I'm selling my home. My parents need the cash and I don't.... They need the money more than I need a house right now." She rolled to her side as best she could without causing her pain. "I'd very much like for you two to leave me alone. I want to take a nap."

The door closed and she knew she was alone. It was in her head that Evan would stay, he'd be that stubborn, but he was gone as well when she turned to look. Her house, the one that she'd been dreaming of owning since she was a kid and had walked by every day to go to school, was gone from her grasp once again. But it was what needed to be done, and the money would go a long way in helping her parents make their monthly obligations.

When she'd called her dad, several months ago now, she'd been down. It had been her birthday. She had no idea why that particular birthday had taken her under, but she had woken with what felt like a black cloud over her and hadn't been able to shake it. Calling her dad and buying the house hadn't helped as much as she had hoped it might. But hearing his voice had lifted her up enough that she could function. Then a few short weeks later, she'd been hurt.

Well, that was a mild term for what had gone down that afternoon. She had been asked what she remembered a couple of times, but since being home, no one had bothered. Hutch was sure that there was going to be some sort of inquiry about it. There wasn't any way that there wouldn't be. Four men had died that day, and several others had been hurt. She'd been lucky, she knew. Ten seconds more where she had been standing and—

"Hello." She looked at the man standing there and nodded at him. He asked if he could have a seat and she pulled out her gun and laid it on the bed where he could see it. "I'm not going to harm you. I swear. I've come to have a little conversation with you. You see, Evan is my grandson."

"Good for you. What the fuck does that have to do with

me?" He laughed and she felt her temper, not in the best place of late, flare up. "I think you should go now."

"He sent me in here because he wanted me to meet you. Talk to you. I've only just found out that he's mated to you. Could have knocked me over with a feather when he told me. I've been sworn to secrecy on it. I don't usually like to keep things from my son, but I thought that this was his story. My Evan has a mate." Hutch shook her head at him. "Oh, but you are, child. You might not have bonded yet, but you're his mate."

"You want grandkids?" He told her that he did, was looking forward to bouncing them on his knee. "I can't give you that. Or him. I've been shot to fuck, and that sort of thing is out of the picture for me. Also, there is some talk that I might not be able to get around without a cane or some sort of support. You understand what I'm trying to tell you? I'm damaged. I nearly died that day."

"But you didn't." There was just no talking to some people, so she sat up. It cost her a great deal, but she wanted this man to see what she'd not even shared with her parents.

"We were just sitting down to eat when we heard the first jet fly over. It was nearly four in the morning our time, and it was a surprise to hear it. The first bomb hit the building next to us. The wall that separated the two buildings came down quickly. The second flyby had us scrambling to get to cover. Gathering what we could, we came out of the building and were sitting ducks." She showed him her legs, then her chest, covering her breasts up as best she could. "Twelve shots to my body before I could take cover after seeing to my men. Then four more to my leg and arms. We tried to return fire but we were low, and outnumbered. The second building came down around us. A part of a wall fell on some of my men, killing one. Then the other walls fell, flames from the bomb burning the flesh off the second part of my squad. Three men died there, another later. I knew as well as they did that we weren't going to make it out."

"I'm sorry." He stood up and she hoped that he was leaving. Perhaps telling his grandson that this was a terrible idea. "Tell me the rest, child. Sometimes getting things off your chest can go a long way into healing the spirit as well as the heart."

She wanted to tell him that was bullshit. How was him knowing the story going to make her walk without a limp? The fact that he'd heard her story would more than likely have him running for home. But Dylan told herself that telling him what had really happened would go a long way into keeping his grandson away from her.

"We were held down for fourteen hours. The enemy was picking us off one at a time. Every time one of us moved, they'd shoot and hit us. There was no one to call…those men were all around us. Just as we were counting out what we had left in ammo, the men shooting at us started to celebrate, yelling and whooping it up like they'd won the war." He took her hand, covering her up with his other one. "I shot one of them. Then another. Killing them while they were enjoying the fact that they'd killed us. But I wasn't going down without a fight."

"Of course you wouldn't. You're a strong, levelheaded young woman. What happened then?" He was humoring her. She didn't know why, but she was going to tell it all to him. "How did you get home?"

"They started returning fire again. We were going to die…I think we all knew that, so we stood there like targets and fired at them. As they started falling, we did as well. After a time, not long, I don't think, they were all dead." He sat back down but held her hand. "The radio was broken, so we had no way of getting anyone to come for us. Just as I was laying down, done for, I guess you could say, this kid comes out of nowhere and points at us. I raised my gun to fire."

"I have heard that they recruit children to help them. I don't know what I would have done if a small one came at me to kill me. You're very brave." She told him she didn't think so. "You are. Many would have given up, let them kill them, but you didn't. Who was she guiding toward you?"

"A tank. The men inside had been sent to find us when they heard that the wall had gone down. It wasn't until they told us we were safe that I realized that I might not make it home at all." He nodded and told her he was glad that she had. "My parents don't know. I'm sure that Evan has it all straight in his head about my injuries, but not how they happened. He thinks, as you do, that we can be mates, but we can't. I'm not whole. I'm not even a nice person on my best days. He'd be better off with some deb than with me."

"I don't think so. And Evan is a good deal smarter than you give him credit for. I bet he knows. And if he doesn't, then you'll need to tell him. Not today. I think telling that story has worn you out." She felt tears fill her eyes and she hated herself for them. This man was making her feel emotions that she'd thought long dead in her heart. "No need for you to get upset, honey. We'll be here for you. And as for children of your own, I'm sure that you will work something out. Or not. Either way, we'll all love you."

"I'm not really the loveable type, Mr. Whitfield." He laughed and told her she was to call him Ollie. "Ollie, in case you didn't notice, I'm not really the type of person that men have hanging on their arm. I'm more of the type that will be just as happy to twist it up behind him for being a jerk."

"Yes, I can see that. Evan said that you were a little on the rough side, but he told me he enjoys that about you. I think he might be right…I enjoy you as well." He laughed again. "You're going to be just right for Evan. Turn up his world a little here and there. My Lizzy, she would have found you to be a little coarse, but she would have loved you too. Responsible, smart girl like you, you'll have him laughing all the time, I'm betting."

"Did you understand what I just told you? That I'm not fit to be a wife for anyone?" He asked her why she would think that. "Because you're a Whitfield and I'm a Hutchinson. You have a new car, I don't own one. I pay my bills by which has the oldest date and which will get me into the most trouble if I let it go another month. My hospital bill here is going to be picked up the Army, but that is about it. I don't have a pot to piss in. Hell, I don't even know if I have a pit that I can take a leak in without someone charging me for it."

"Yes, I'm a Whitfield. So will you be too, soon enough, if I know Evan. You don't ever have to worry about money again, not so long as you and Evan are good with what you have. For all I know, Evan might not ever have to work again, but that's not something I'm privy too. You have bills?" She shook her head. "Yeah, didn't think so. Like I said, you're a responsible person and you'd give something up in order to pay your responsibilities on time. I like that about you. You're going to be good for him. And for us if I don't miss my bet."

Hutch wanted to get angry with him, but he was just too

cute. She'd bet anything that his wife let him get by with a great many things when she was alive. He was a charmer too. When he sat back in the chair, still holding her hand, she squeezed it tightly and asked him if he was going to be around for a while.

"I surely am. I moved in with my son and his wife the other week. I had me a home but it was too much for me. And the memories were a little hard. I sold it to Evan. You'll love it there." She said that she doubted it if Evan was going to be there. He was still laughing at her as he described the house to her.

~~~

Evan heard them laughing when he was outside her door. His grandpa was the only person he'd told about Dylan, and it seemed like he was right in asking him to talk to her. As soon as he opened the door, the smell of fresh blood hit his nose and he looked at Dylan.

"It's fine. I just moved funny when talking to your grandda." He asked if he could have a look. "No. I just told you I was fine. Why do you forever want to do just the opposite of what I tell you?"

"I'm a doctor." She asked him how that was supposed to be an answer. "It's the only one I have. Now, lie back so I can have a look."

His grandpa stood up. "I'm gonna go now, Hutch. You have a nice evening, and remember what I told you." She told him she would and he kissed her on the cheek. When they were alone, Evan had her lie back so he could get a better look.

"You and my grandpa seemed to get along." She hissed at him when he touched his fingers to one of the wounds on her belly. "I'm sorry. The stitches are pulled, but I think you'll be all

57

right for a bit. Just don't do anything quickly and I won't have to redo them. What did my grandpa mean?"

"He was talking to me, not you. And I didn't have any plans of doing anything quickly, except get away from you." Still sour, he saw. "He's a nice man. Why didn't you get any of that from him?"

"I'm a nice man. You just bring out the worst in me. And I'm sure that if you had to spend much time with him, you'd be just as cranky with him." She told him he'd been there since breakfast. "That long? I just told him to pop by and get to know you. He's been in a funk lately."

"He told me. Ollie said he lost his wife recently." Evan sat in the chair his grandpa had been in. "Don't get comfortable. You're not staying that long."

"You're forever pushing me away. Why is that? Do I have bad breath? Do you not like my cologne?" She told him he wasn't wearing any. "And how do you know that?"

"I've been trained to smell out the enemy, as well as listen for them." Evan asked her if he was the enemy. "You are so long as you believe that I can be your mate. I've told you, repeatedly now, that we're nothing to each other. I'm not your mate."

"You are." Evan wanted to crawl into the bed with her. He wanted to touch her skin to his. To hold her. "I hired a crew to come out and clean the house for us. I'm thinking that for the time being, we'll have a bedroom set up for us on the lower level. I don't have to sleep with you yet, but you'll be able to get around more comfortably that way."

"The house that I owned was beautiful too. Ollie described the one he sold you. It's close to where I had one." He asked her which house. "The blue one on the corner from yours. It's the big one that used to be an antique store."

"I remember that house. Yes, that is a lovely old home. Would you prefer to live in that one?" She told him it was on the market now. "I could buy it. And sell Grandpa's. I think that Adam wanted to buy it anyway."

"No, I don't want you to buy it. And I don't want you to do anything with your house that you don't want to. My parents are going to need the money for bills and things." He didn't say anything and she laid her head back. "Why are you here? I thought you were going to go to your parents' or something."

"I am, for dinner. But I wanted to come by and see you before I left. How would you like to go there next weekend?" She eyed him, and he nearly laughed at the hopeful look on her face. "You won't be able to get around very much, but we could set you up at the table and you could enjoy dinner with us. Grandpa will be there too."

"If you let me go from here, I really should be at my own parents' home." She wanted to go, he could see it on her face. He wished she looked at him the way she looked right now. "Your grandpa, he said that your mom goes all out when you guys are home for dinner. I've not eaten with my family in decades."

"That's so sad. But you're home now, so you can see them more." Dylan nodded and he thought of something. "My grandpa, he called you Hutch. I think Randy did that as well. I understand where it came from, but not why anyone calls you that."

"Hutchinson is a little long when you're working with a bunch of people. Hutch was easier to say. There was also a man named Charlie. His last name was Charleston. First name was....

59

I don't remember, but he got his name shortened as well." Evan watched her doze in and out. When she yawned again, he did as well. "I'd like to be alone now. I'm exhausted."

"I am as well. It's been a very long day." She nodded and dozed again.

Evan loved watching her body relax, her arms that were usually so tense seemed to fall to the side. When he was sure she was asleep, he went to the bed to touch her.

She was warm, her skin was soft. He'd noticed that her hands were callused the other day, and wondered what she'd done to get them that way. He knew so very little about her. Moving the chair closer to the bed, he sat down and held her hand in his as he thought of all the things he was going to do now.

He thought about her home, the one that she'd bought and then sold. He knew that she'd done it from love...her dad had told him that he really hated to see her sell it for them. Norris told him how she'd been saving her money for a very long time to get herself one, to live with her grandda. He wondered if Adam would buy Grandpa's so that Evan could get the one that she really wanted. He messaged Adam, also telling him that she was his mate.

Just as he got his phone put on mute, Adam replied. He told him congratulations. Yes, he'd love to buy the house, and yes, he thought it a great idea to buy the other for Hutch. It occurred to him that his family didn't know about her being his mate yet, and decided to tell them tonight.

"*You coming to dinner?*" He told his brother that he was. "*I have it on good authority that you could take her too. I mean, don't you have one of those early release programs?*"

60

"*I never thought of that. She'll enjoy it, I think.*" Adam sent him a happy face. "*I'll get back with you. She's resting now.*"

"*Good. I'll see you in a couple hours then.*" Adam then told him to tread slowly before he got himself killed. Good advice, he thought, and went to find a nurse.

By the time he was finished, Evan felt like he'd been holding national secrets. The guard outside of her room had to contact Randy, who had to contact his boss, and so on. Someone was also going to go to the house with them, and stay until she was well enough to walk on her own, as well as someone in their household forever. Or so it sounded like to him. He had remembered at the last minute to tell his parents, and they suggested that they invite the Hutchinsons en masse. He thought that was both scary as well as a good idea. Now he had to tell Dylan.

Waking her seemed simple until he was standing close to her. Her scent was soft, calling to him in a very carnal way. But it was her mouth that seemed to beckon him the most. Begging him to taste her. To sample the riches that he knew were there. Evan also knew, however, that lurking somewhere under her blanket was a gun, and she wasn't the least bit afraid to use it. So instead of giving into what he really wanted, he touched his hand to her shoulder. The pain took his breath away before he could think touching Dylan was bad no matter what you did.

CHAPTER 5

Hutch looked over at Evan, and had to hold back a laugh as they rode to his house in the limo. He had blood on his shirt, and his tie was torn. There was some blood on his nose too, but that wasn't what made her laugh. It was the fact that he was embarrassed. She had no idea why, but it was funny to her that a man could be so confident about everything, but her taking him down had upset him.

"You know, I think you should be a little sorry for what you did." She asked him why. "Because, I was waking you up to bring you to my house. You have no idea what I had to go through to get that to happen."

"Yeah, well, I was sleeping and you woke me suddenly. I'm used to springing to action when something startles me. What would you have done had I come up with a gun instead of my fists?" He mumbled something. "What was that? I didn't understand with your lip all pouted out like it is."

"I wondered if you'd be like that when we're sleeping together." He looked at her then, his eyes full of hunger, his cat right there where she could see it. "Of course, I don't think we'll be sleeping that much. At least I hope not. I'd like to take you

63

now, have you ride me while we're sitting here on this seat."

Her body burned with the thought of having sex with this man. He'd be good at it too…nothing soft and easy about him. Evan would give her everything she'd ever hoped for from making love to someone. Not the fumbles in the dark that she was used to getting. Trying hard not to think about him, she countered with meanness, something she was very good at.

"What makes you think that I'd like to have sex with you?" He jerked her to him, careful even in his hurry not to hurt her. When she was sitting across his lap, she felt his cock, thick and hard between her thighs. "You're not playing fairly, Evan. What if I'm a screamer and I shout out your name loud enough that everyone in the front of this limo can hear me?"

"I don't care, and they'd be happy that we're finally a couple. Are you a screamer? Also, I could care less if anyone hears you coming to peak. The fact that you're coming on me while riding me will make me indifferent to any kind of noises you think you may make." She rolled her hips, careful of her wounds too. "Do that again. I want to taste you when you come like this."

"And what about you? Don't you want to enjoy a little fun too?" He grinned at her. "I don't think I care for that look on you. You looked like.... Well, you remind me of the cat eating the canary."

"I won't eat the canary, darling, but you. Would you let my cat have his fill of you too? Lick you until you come? I'd very much like that. Having you spread out before me, your lush body naked and covered in your dewy need." She felt her pussy swell, her body heat all over. "I need to taste your breasts. Give them to me."

Lifting her bra up with her shirt, she felt his breath on her. It was all she could do not to beg him for more. To tell him to take her right now. And when his tongue lapped at her nipple so that it tightened, she cried out when he blew his breath over the dampness of it.

"Please. I need you to take me." He growled, the cat moving over his skin so that she could see his fur. "Make me come, Evan. Please? I need that."

He took her whole breast into his mouth. She held him to her, her fingers tight in his hair while she did. When he caught her nipple between his teeth, she came apart, her body bowing back against his hands as he held her. And when he told her to come again, she did so, thinking that much more of him and she'd be dead. Then he bit down on her.

It was painful, yet fulfilling. And when he sucked hard, making her breast ache for more, she yanked his head away and took his mouth. Christ, kissing him was a great deal like what she thought it would be. It was like sticking her finger into a socket while standing in water. It was consuming and completely unfamiliar to her. But by far the best feeling that she'd felt in her entire life.

He moved his mouth along her collarbone, her ear lobe, and her neck. Each place his tongue touched her, his teeth nipped at her, and she felt like she'd been branded, her body marked as his. It was too much for her, yet not enough. This man was going to make her feel like no one ever had before. And when he bit her throat, she died inside for a moment...her body simply stopped functioning.

The scream along with the release came from her feet. It consumed her, the knowledge of him taking her blood into his body. And when he pulled her pussy to his cock, she rode him hard, faster and faster, until she came again. As he continued to suckle at her, his body rocking upward into hers, she wanted to taste him in the same way he had her, and begged him to let her.

"Bite hard. Draw blood." She nodded, her head dizzy with coming so hard, her need making her reckless and single minded. "When you taste me, Dylan, you belong to no one but me."

"Please. I need this."

He nodded and tipped his head for her. His cock seemed to have stretched, and she reached down and unbuttoned his jeans. When he sat up, pulling them down to his thighs, she came again. The pants she had on were shredded in seconds, and she didn't care.

His cock was thick, the crown of him so wide that she wondered if he'd fit inside her. But she didn't care if he tore her open, so long as he filled her. And when she lowered herself over him, his cock filling her completely, she licked the pulse at his throat and felt him stiffen.

"Come with me, Dylan. Come when I do and we'll be one forever." Hutch wasn't sure she had anything left in her to come again…she was weak with it now. But when he took her breast into his mouth once more, thumbing the hard bud on the other, she felt her body rejuvenate, her heartrate triple.

When his head tilted again, she licked him there, feeling the pounding pulse under her tongue like a ticking time bomb. And when he came, screaming out his release at her breast, she joined him even as she bit down as hard as she could at his throat.

The climax took her under for a moment...her body burned with it, her mind ran circles in her head as if something was different and it was searching out the problem. Then she realized what it was, what had happened when she'd bitten him.

The connection was immediate and profound. She knew his thoughts, his memories, as well as his love. She wondered at that, just for a moment, when she realized that he'd have her memories as well. That he'd know things about her that no one else did. Laying her head on his shoulder, she tried to think what that would mean for him.

Not that she wanted him in her life. But there were personal things, things that she'd done, how she'd done them, that were a part of her job. Killing men and women when necessary. Kidnapping someone when they had information that she had needed. And her loneliness at being so far from home. She looked down at him when he said her name.

"You're not alone now." She nodded, and he helped her move to the seat beside him. Nodding when he said it again, she turned away, but he pulled her chin around to look at him. "I'm sorry that you feel that way, I really am, but you aren't alone. Not ever again."

"You know, better than most, what sort of person I am." He nodded, but didn't say anything. "You saw them. My memories. Doesn't that make you want to run in the other direction? To break this off before it's too late for you?"

"It's already too late, and I have no intention of breaking it off with you. Not now, not ever. Your memories, those things you did, they were done to keep you alive. To save you for me. You're a good person, I can see that as well." She wasn't getting through to him and it pissed her off. Before she could take action, not even sure what that was, he smiled at her. "You don't have any pants to wear. I'm not sure, but I'm betting that someone will notice your lack of attire. My grandpa, he'll comment on it first, then the rest of them will. It'll be an all out—"

"Christ. First impression with your parents and family is going to be a fuck up. What the hell am I supposed to do without pants? Tell them what we've done here?" He said that they would already know. "Damn it. What the fuck? Did you already tell them? I know that you can.... Please tell me that you didn't already shout it to the fucking world that we had sex."

"No, I didn't. And as much as I'd like to, they'll know by being able smell me on you. As well as you on me." It took her a second or two to realize what he was saying, and she felt her face heat up. "Well, I never expected to see you embarrassed. That's sort of adorable—"

She grabbed his naked cock and squeezed. The look on his face went from agony to pure pleasure in a few heartbeats. And when he rocked upward in her hand, she leaned over him and took him into her mouth.

"Holy Christ." She could taste herself on him. His cum was there as well, and she moaned at the flavor. When he pulled her up from him, his face a concentration in pain, she tried to go back to what she was doing and he stopped her. "Dylan, we've forgotten for a moment where we are...at my parents' house in their driveway. Right now, as much as I'd like for you to continue this—need for you to, actually—we can't. Christ. They're wondering why we're taking so long to get out of the car as it is."

She'd forgotten that they were in the car, and headed to

his parents'. The only thought that she'd had in her head was taking this man, making him take her too. And now that they were stopped, the limo still, she wanted to murder him as well as herself. What the fuck had gotten into her? Well, he had, but that wasn't the point. Glaring at him, she took her anger out on him.

"You're going to pay for this. What am I supposed to do now?" He adjusted his pants, moaning when he had to move his cock twice to push the snaps together. Then he handed her a large duffle.

"There should be a pair of pants in there. And some T-shirts. We'll have to.... Do you have any idea what I'd like to do to you right now? And this limo will never be the same again when I'm finished with you."

Instead of answering him, she buried her face in the bag. If there was clothing in the thing, she never saw it. Her eyes were filled with tears, stupid ones that she had no idea why they were there. Grabbing the first thing she touched, she pulled on the pants and knew that they were going to be way too big for her. But when she opened the door to get away from him, she was stopped by the pain that shot through her body.

~~~

Eve watched the couple. There was no doubt that neither of them had any idea what they were to do now, but it was fun watching them. Evan was out of his league with the young woman. Not that he didn't know how to treat the opposite sex, but this one wasn't taking to his charm and wit. And poor Dylan was on pins and needles, trying her best to behave and not curse like Eve was sure she could. And quite well too, she thought, judging by the way she'd torn into Evan when they'd gotten out of the limo and she'd hurt herself.

"I love potatoes." She looked at Bailey and asked him if he wanted some more. "No. I'd better not. I don't want to eat too much and not have dessert."

He was so childlike now. When he'd first gotten to their home, he was both combative and terrified. Then Evan had shown up and he changed in a moment. There was a friendship there that she approved of for both of them. It seemed that Evan was a balm for the older man, and the same was true for Evan. They clicked, she supposed was the perfect word for them.

"We have homemade ice cream with peaches, as well as cobbler. I think there is a peach one of those, as well as cherry. The trees are doing well this year." Bailey told her that he thought he liked peach. "I do as well. But the boys all prefer cherry. That's why I make them both. I'm so glad I have someone to share it with."

She liked the Hutchinsons. All of them. Even Stella, who was a little overwhelmed, Eve thought, when she'd first came in. Now she was doing better, but was not calm yet. Twice she'd tried to bring her into the conversation, but she would murmur something and then lower her head. Eve wasn't sure what she had to do to bring her out of her shell, but Norris had no such trouble talking.

"Before I forget, my dad needs a puppy. I was wondering how we could make that work and not have any trouble again." Norris told him about the big dog earlier, and his reactions to the scent his dad had carried. "I don't want to be rude about it, and I hope that you don't mind me asking."

"No. It's fine. In fact, we have a litter of pups on the ranch right now. Kittens too. Though the kittens are wild for the most part, but if we go with you, there isn't any reason that you couldn't hold them." Oliver winked at her as he continued. "The pups are about ready to leave their momma. If you'd like to go out there and pick one out, we'd be more than glad to let you have one. They're used to us."

"I'm sure that Dad would love that." Norris looked at his dad. "Dad, how about after supper, we go and have a look at the pups? You can take one home if you want."

"I'd like that. I really would." He sat there staring at his plate, then looked at Eve. She was sure that he was lost again, and his next words confirmed it. "I have to go to the bathroom. I don't remember where it is. I've been trying to hold it until I remembered, but I just don't know if I can any more."

His voice was low, like a small child afraid of the adults taking him to task. But before she could tell him that she'd take him, Evan stood up and said he'd do it. When they were out of the room, she looked around the table, then at Stella.

"If you ever need help, a break or someone to talk to, you should call." Stella said she was fine. "No, you're not. You're stressed out and terrified. Of us. I want you to know that I'd enjoy having a friend in you. Now that the kids are a couple, we'll be seeing a...."

"Hold your horses. I didn't say we were a couple." Eve turned and looked at Dylan. The woman was nearly standing when she sat back down. "I'm a little on the lightheaded side, but not that off the mark. He said we were mates, nothing more. I don't have time for even that much, but he's pretty persuasive."

"I'm sure that you both are." Eve laughed when Dylan turned red. "Oh, Dylan, you're going to be so good for us all, I think. You're a delight, and as I was telling your mother, I think that we'll all get along just fine now."

"She's thinking that we won't want her because of some injuries that she has." Eve looked at her father-in-law and he told her what he meant. "She and I, we had a nice long conversation the other day. Hutch here has it in her head that we're going to turn her out on account'a her having scars and such."

"I don't just have scars and such, but I can't have children. And they're saying that I can't return to work." Eve was disappointed, yes, but more so for the girl, not the fact that she'd not be a grandma. "I've got some healing to do. I've taken some major hits to my body recently."

"We weren't thinking you'd be a broodmare, child, but to be happy with Evan and have a good life." Eve kicked her husband under the table. "What was that for? Goodness, I was just telling her that we don't care if she has biological children or not so long as they're happy."

"You could have been a little more tactful about it, Oliver Whitfield. Not calling her a horse might have been a little nicer as well." She turned to Dylan, hoping that she would understand and not be upset. "Dylan, there are any number of children you can adopt. If you'd like, that is. I know there are four children right now being taken from their home because of.... Well, they're not in a safe place. Evan knows them. I think they're going into the system soon." Evan sat down with Bailey as Eve was telling them about the children. "They've been hurt a great deal too. Not so much physically, but words harm too."

"The Franklin children?" Eve told Evan what they'd been speaking about when he nodded and continued. "They're human. Their father is going to prison for a very long time. The mother is having some issues, and will be hospitalized for more than likely the rest of her life. The kids, they're relieved, I think, to be left to their own devices."

"You're all acting like this is no big deal." Eve said that if she thought they were upset, then she shouldn't because worse things could be happening. "But he'll never be a father of his own child. Doesn't that bother you?"

"No." Everyone turned to Evan when he spoke. "All I've ever wanted in my life was someone to love. That would be you. I would love children, and hope we have them someday. But just because they wouldn't be of your body or mine would make them no less our children. Being with you, loving them with you, that's much more important than anything else in this world to me."

Eve watched Dylan struggle with this information. She'd bet anything that someone had said something to her. Something about her inability to have children and hurt her. Dylan had little trust, it seemed, and they'd have to work hard at making sure that she trusted each of them. Standing up, she asked who wanted pie.

She was standing at the counter trying to think what she'd have to do when her father-in-law touched her shoulder. Eve loved this old man…he irritated her to no end, but she loved him. When he turned her and hugged her, Eve hadn't realized how much she'd needed that until then.

"She's been hurt." He said he knew that from their conversation the other day. "We need to make her happy, Ollie. I don't think she has been in a long while."

"Evan will make her happy again. We'll be there for them both, too. I think…I believe that she feels herself unworthy. Not

73

just of Evan, but of life in general." She looked up at him. "She was coming home soon to take care of her grandfather, to give her parents a break, and this happened. She's had to sell her home to provide for them. Randy, her CO, told me that she'll be paid for her services for the rest of her life, but she's taking that hard as well. Not working and being paid is equivalent to being a deadbeat to her."

"That poor girl." Ollie told her about the house that Evan had bought. "I thought he was buying your house. What's he going to do about that one?"

"Adam wanted it, from what he was telling me, I think he was going to buy it anyway, and Evan beat him to the draw. Good for them. I think being homeowners will be nice for them all, don't you think? It's high time, Eve, that you kicked those boys to the curb and let them get their own homes." She'd actually been thinking the same thing, but hadn't wanted them to think her a terrible mom for kicking them out on their own. "You want me to do it? I'd be as happy as a clam to help. Them boys, they mean the world to me, and so do you and my son. They need to spread out them wings they've clipped by staying with you."

"I never wanted them to be stifled." He told her she was seeing it all wrong. "But you said I had to kick them out. What am I supposed to take from that?"

"Now, don't be going and getting yourself all twisted up. I think they love being with you and their dad. More than they do living alone. But it's all on them, not you. They love their momma too much to move out." She nodded, but didn't look happy. "If they're not here, you supposing that they'll all find themselves mates? I mean, it's hard to test the waters with

Momma right outside their doors."

"Oliver Patrick Whitfield." He laughed. "What a thing to say to me. My boys would.... Oh. You mean they're not getting out because they live at home. I see. Yes. I think you're absolutely right. They need to be out on their own. But not too far. I still need them close."

"Of course you do. So do I, now that I'm...I'm alone. I miss her every day." She told him she did as well. "With the boys getting hitched up and having babies, it'll be a sight better, I think, being alone. And having us some grandkids? Well, I don't know what I'm gonna do about that, but I sure am going to be happy figuring it out. To think, we might have some babies around again. And maybe a few more little girls like Dylan."

"You're not alone, you old fool. What are we, chopped liver? You go on back in there and I'll be bringing in the pies. And if you think you've buttered me up enough that you can have two pieces, then you're wrong." He kissed her on the cheek and took the churn of ice cream with him. "That man is going to make me crazy, that's what he's going to do."

Cutting the three pies up, she was just gathering up the plates and forks when Joshua came to help. She was worried about this son of hers. He'd been moping about for a couple of weeks now. Handing him the plates, she held his hands as he stood there.

"I love you." He told her that he loved her too. "I want you to find you a lovely home. Make it perfect for you, and go out on more dates."

"Where on earth did that come from?" He laughed a little. "You have one son mated, and you're trying to push the rest of us into it now, right?"

"Yes." He looked shocked. "But it wouldn't hurt you to have a nice home, would it? Your father and I, we're not getting any younger. And we would love to see you all out and about, not hanging around us old folks."

"You'll never be old, Mom. And I've actually been thinking about a house myself." She smiled, while inside her heart was breaking at the thought, thinking it was too soon. "It's the property in the meadow. I'd like to build on it. Would you and Dad sell it to me? Not give, but sell. If I'm doing to do this, I'm going to do it right."

"I think we can do that for you. In fact, we should split things up for all you boys. Evan and Adam both have a home now, so perhaps we can think of something else for them." Joshua said he had an idea. "Good. Let's have lunch tomorrow. Can you arrange that?"

"For the love of my life, I can always manage anything." She smacked him on the chest and told him to go. He turned and looked at her when she had the pies. "Mom, I don't tell you this often enough, but I love you with all my heart, and will no matter if I find a mate or not."

"Thank you, son. And when you find her, I hope she makes you happy, just as happy as you boys have me my whole life."

She needed a minute after he left her. The thought of her boys growing up and leaving her was both heartbreaking as well as exciting. She'd have to find some things in the barn to give to them that had been in the family for generations. They'd like that, she thought.

Things were moving now; the boys were becoming men. She knew that they were already, but now they were acting like it. It broke her heart, yes, but it made her feel good too.

She'd done her part in raising them to be good, dependable men. Now it was going to be up to any woman that wanted to love them too to make them theirs. She only hoped they were as wonderful as Dylan was. Eve was sure that they would be.

Chapter 6

Dylan wasn't sure what she was supposed to be doing. The room she'd been put in was obviously Evan's, but where did they think she was going to sleep? She looked up at him when he came out of the bathroom.

"You okay?" She nodded, then shook her head. "Yeah, right there with you, I'm afraid. I thought that my mom would put us in separate rooms. I'm glad that we're here, but it's weird. I think she's trying to be modern thinking."

"I think your parents are amazing. My mom was so impressed with them that she said she wished they'd met earlier." Evan sat on the bed she'd been put on when he'd carried her up here. "I'm terrified, if you want to know the truth."

"About what? Us? We're doing fine, Dylan. We'll work this out." She shook her head, then nodded. "Tell me what's wrong."

"I'm not like you." Evan said that was what made them a perfect couple. Male and female. "No, you ass, I'm not used to having people bow before me because I've got money. I don't know how to act when you tell me that what you have is mine too. I've been...well, since I was about sixteen, I've always worked and made my own way in the world. Now you're telling me that I'm as rich as you are, and I haven't any idea what that means."

"If you're talking net worth, then we're pretty close to being billionaires. We have money in all kinds of investments. I've bought up some properties that have a nice income, as well as a couple of homes around the world. My family has had money for generations." She told him that wasn't what she meant, and wished that he'd not told her. "Okay, then you explain to me and I'll try and answer. All right?"

"You're really a billionaire?" He laughed and told her *they* were. "You see? That's it right there. I'm not a billionaire. I'm me. An injured sergeant from the Army who likes organization, rules, and calmness. I get a check each month that goes into an account to help out my mom and dad. I do not know how to be one of those rich and fabulous people you see on television."

"You'll never be like them, honey. As far as rules and organizing, you can have that too. I like organization and rules as well. I doubt there will be much in the way of calmness, but we can try. What is it you'd like to do? I mean, if you could do something that you think would fulfil you, what would that be?" She told him she had no idea. "Come on, love. There must be something that you think you'd be wonderful at."

"I'm wonderful at everything." They both laughed and she laid back on the bed. "I've been in the service all my entire adult life. I don't know anything else. I thought about going to college, but I have no idea what I'd study. I was going to enjoy my grandda while he was still around, but I can't do that now either not for a while yet."

"Oh. Before I forget, I sold Adam my grandpa's house, and I bought the one you owned before. It was still in escrow, so they were willing and ready to get it off the books before it sat empty again." She just stared at him. "It's a good investment and a nice sized house. I've not been in it yet. I thought we'd go through it in a couple of days to find out what we'll need in the way of furniture."

"You're nuts." He grinned. "You bought a house without going through it, and you now want to furnish it. What if it needs work? I'm sure it does. It's been empty for about two decades." He told her someone was going through it tomorrow to see if it needed any renovations. "Just like that."

"Yes. You loved that house. I needed one, and this worked out not only for us, but Adam as well. He was going to take Grandpa's house when I beat him to it. And he's moving in soon. He said that we can have any of the furniture that's in there that he doesn't want." It was going too fast and she told him that. "You're going to need a few more weeks of therapy before you can walk without as much pain. And there is the fact that Mom said she'd help you by taking you back and forth to the hospital when I'm at work. Which reminds me, I need to get you something to drive."

"Slow the fuck down." He smiled at her. "You don't have to buy me a car. Nor do you need to make arrangements for me to have my ass carted all over the place. I can take care of myself."

"You can, I have no doubt about that. But you can't drive yet, not with your arm and legs still giving you pain." She nodded...there was that. "And my mom wants to get to know you better. I think her words were to welcome you to the family."

"I'm not their family. I'm not even sure about this thing with us." He kissed her, pulling her to him and planting a deep sizzling one on her mouth. When she was let go, she stared at him for several seconds before speaking. "Do you have any idea what you're getting in me? I mean, aside from the injuries, I'm a pain in the ass. Vulgar, rude, and opinionated. Why the hell would you want me in your life? Not to mention, I have no idea how to be a rich man's plaything."

"First of all, I plan to make you my wife when I can get you to say yes. You can still be my plaything, but my wife first and foremost." She told him he'd not asked. "Will you marry me?"

"No, I won't. But go on, tell me your reasons for thinking that I should be here with you." He kissed her again. This one was short but no less hot. "Evan, you need to be serious about this. We're not suited."

"The fates think that we are. You were born just for me." She snorted at him. "Well, believe it or not, I think you're perfect for me. And as for the other things you mentioned, yes. You are slightly vulgar. Rude? I don't know. I've seen you be as sweet as my mom's pie when you want to be. As for being a pain in the ass, well, I hate to tell you this, but I don't think you are. You could be, I suppose, but you're not usually. Unless we're talking about when you're upset with me. I don't know why you'd be that way…I don't think you've realized how perfect I am just yet."

"Sure you are. And I'm a debutante. What if one of your rich friends asks you or me what I did for a living? I'm sure that it will go over quite well that I was a sergeant in the Army and got shot to fuck when out on a mission once." He said no one would care. "Are you sure about that? I've killed people. Done things that, while I'm not ashamed of them, people will think are wrong."

"I don't care. I mean, I care if they bother you about it, but what you did was what made you what you are today." She shook her head. He wasn't getting it. "I do get it, Dylan. I love you."

"You can't love me, Evan. You don't know me." He said nothing. "You're making me insane, you know that, don't you? Why is it you think your word is law? Huh? I'm not suited to you."

"Yes, you are. And you're doing the same to me." He stretched and started pulling off his shirt. "I'm exhausted. You wore me out in the limo. Now, if there are no more excuses, I'd like to get some rest so I can wake you in the morning by sliding deep into your body."

He stripped down to his skin. She stared at him for several seconds before he turned out the light. As soon as he curled his big warm body around hers, she closed her eyes. She'd have a serious conversation with him in the morning, damn it. And he'd listen to her this time.

When she woke, the room was flooded with light. Hutch lay there for several minutes before she realized that not only was she alone in the big bed, but in the room as well. Wondering what had happened, she started to sit up when she saw the note on the bedside table beside her. Picking it up, she read the note.

"Morning, darling. I'm sorry that I'm not there when you wake, but I got an emergency call at one and had to go in. I don't know how long I'll be, but hopefully sometime before lunch. If not, I'll see you at dinner. Love, E."

What was she supposed to do now, she wondered? Hutch was still unable to care for a lot of things on her own...getting up was sometimes too painful for her. But when she sat up, thinking that she'd crawl to the bathroom, she was amazed at how easy it was. Standing required a little more work and there was some pain, but not like before. Holding onto the walls and furniture, she made her way to the bathroom. With each step, she felt a little stronger, a little less stiff than she normally did.

Turning on the shower might have been a bit optimistic, but she really wasn't hurting all that much. After getting undressed, she held onto the wall and stepped into the warm water. It was the first shower she'd had in months, and she moaned at the feeling of the water all over her.

It took her more time than normal to clean up. She washed her hair three times, simply because she could. Scrubbed her body harder than she should have, if the soreness of it was any indication, but when she turned off the water and reached for a towel, Hutch felt better than she had in months. Like a new person.

She dressed in more of Evan's clothing. His pants were way too big for her, but she found some jogging pants that she could cinch up. There were all colors of shirts in his drawers, some of them with name brand logos. Taking one that had nothing on it but the name of a college, she sat down to rest. Closing her eyes, she wondered if this had been such a good idea.

The knock at the door startled her awake, and she bid the person on the other side to come in. When she saw Eve there, she sat up straighter in the chair and pulled her hair off her face. Eve went to the bathroom and brought her back a brush to use.

"I heard the water turn on, then you were taking so long

I got worried. I'm glad to see you up and about. How do you feel?" She told her that she was better than she had been in some time. "That's wonderful. I'm so glad to hear that. If you'd like, I was just going to have a cup of tea and a light snack. If you think you can make it down the stairs, we can enjoy that together."

"I'm not much for tea. I drink coffee when I can, but tea isn't something that I've grown fond of over the years." Eve said that they could handle that as well. "May I ask you a question? You don't have to answer if you don't want, but why are you being so nice to me? Evan and I, we might not make it as a couple. We're trying things out. But, you've been really nice to me regardless of how nasty I am to him and how much I curse."

"You're going to find that he might have told you that he'd try things out, but for shifters and other paranormals, once we find our mates, it's a done deal." She said she'd heard that, but she wasn't a shifter. "No, not yet at any rate. Evan could change you, but that would be up to the two of you. But it matters little if you're a shifter or not, child. You're his mate, and you'll be with him forever. If not...well, if you leave him and he can't follow, or you come up missing, he'll not survive."

"That can't be true. I mean, Ollie is still around and he's doing all right." Eve nodded and helped her stand after she got her hair in a ponytail. "And what do you mean, he'll not survive?"

"Ollie is doing all right now, but a few weeks ago he was ready to step in front of a bus. Or any other fast moving vehicle. He wanted to join his mate so badly that we all worried for him. Then he spoke to Evan. I don't know what the conversation was about, not fully, but the next afternoon, not only did he

85

sell his house and move in with us, he also got a new start on life." Hutch asked her what had happened. "You did, my dear. You gave him a reason to move forward instead of backwards. Now, are you ready to tackle these stairs? If not, I can have one of the boys help. They're packing their things up."

"You've kicked them out?" She said that she had. "Well, good for you. I mean, it's wonderful that you've let them live here for so long, but you have to be cramping their love life just a little. I'm sure they were getting around that, but it'll be good for them to have a place of their own."

"I thought so as well. However, I don't want to think of any of my sons having sex. It's just too weird." Hutch was down three steps when she laughed. "Ollie told me that I have to cut the apron strings. It was much easier than I thought it would be. Of course, they'll be close to us. Joshua is building so he'll be living in town, but not that far. And now that you and Evan have a home being worked on, I'll see you too."

"I bet that hurt you too. Cutting the strings as you called it." She told her it did, a little. "Yeah. While you want them to have a life, you don't want them to forget that you're around. My mom said that to me when I left for a tour. It was easier on her, I think. I had been pushing away for a long time. And they had Grandda to contend with. He wasn't as bad as he is now, but he was getting there. I'm sure that me leaving was sort of a help for them, one less thing they had to worry about. But they did, especially after I'd been hurt."

By the time she was down the stairs, she was exhausted again. After taking her to the living room and helping her sit on the couch, Eve left to get them some lunch. Closing her eyes again, Hutch let exhaustion take her. It was going better than she had hoped for, but it was very tiring.

~~~

Evan was just closing his eyes when his brother contacted him. Joshua had been redoing houses since he was a teenager, and Evan had asked him to go over the house. He wasn't worried that it was unfit, he could see that much, but he wondered about things like the furnace, hot water heater, and such.

I'm going to see the house this morning, but I have the specs on it and thought I'd give you those first. As far as the electrical work goes, it's been redone recently and inspected. Someone even took the time to add more plugs in each room when the walls were redone. Everything was done well. He asked him about the furnace. *You'll need to update it soon. If it were me, I'd do it now before winter, and have the air and new duct work done as well. That way you won't lose heat or cold when you need it most.*

Good to know. I got pictures of the kitchen and the rest of the house from the realtor that sold it to Dylan, so I know it needs a new update in there. Also, I think the bathrooms are a little outdated. Joshua told him they were. *And the plumbing? How's that going to hold up?*

Believe it or not, it's in great shape. When I was talking to someone about the house, they said that the original owners, before Dylan, had wanted to update the whole house, but they ran out of money when they put in the new plumbing. This was some time ago, but it was state of the art then and hasn't been used since it was put in. I think the kitchen was next on their to do list to do next. But, even had they done it, I'm sure that it would have been outdated again by now. It's been sitting empty for a couple of decades since then. Evan watched the nurses come in and out of the room he was in, and asked after his patient. When he was told there was no change, Joshua continued. *You'll need new carpets or hardwood flooring. There is also an elevator in the back of the house that is in excellent shape. And beautiful, from what I've been told. Kitchen is really dated as you said, bathrooms need an overhaul too. While it sounds like a great deal to take on, you should know that the house is in excellent shape. Sturdy and sound. I'm going over there in an hour.*

If I'm done here, maybe I can go with you. My patient is going to pull through and I can leave here for a bit, but I'll have to come back. Joshua said that he'd work around his schedule. *Thanks. Let me take another look, then I'll have a better idea as to when I can go.*

Forty-five minutes later they were pulling up in front of the house. Evan was glad that he'd been able to get in touch with his grandpa, and he was going to bring Dylan with him to see the house as well. He'd not realized that she'd only ever been on the outside of the house when she'd bought it, and never inside. He was excited to have her tour it with him.

When Dylan went in the house before him, he looked at her. There was something.... He wasn't sure what it was, but he looked over at his grandpa when he laughed. Evan felt his face heat up when he thought of what his grandpa might be thinking.

"She's getting around all right now, don't you think?" Evan looked at Dylan as she moved toward the right. "I noticed it right off when she came down the stairs this morning. It was hard for me to recognize it for what it was, but I'm thinking that she won't need that cane thing much longer, don't you?"

"What happened?" This time his face felt like it had been set on fire. All Grandpa did was shake his head and he knew. "Sex? Are you saying that sex made her better?"

"No, but that can't hurt either of you. I'm thinking that you gave her a little bit of yourself. Did you exchange blood?" He nodded. "Well, there you go. Helped her right along. And if you keep it up, you'll fix her so she'll be as good as new."

He was still standing on the porch when Dylan came out of the room she'd been in and stared at him. Evan had heard that his blood, all their blood, was powerful, but he'd never thought of what it might do for someone like Dylan. When she asked him if he was coming in, he did. Reaching for her hand, he clasped it as they went through their new home.

The kitchen would have to be gutted and rebuilt from scratch. It would be easier, his brother told him, than to try and swap out pieces as they needed them. That was fine with him. Evan liked to cook, but he didn't think that he'd enjoy doing it every meal. They'd hire a cook and someone to clean the place, for sure. He looked at the pantry when Dylan asked him to.

"There's a freezer in here. Why on earth would someone put in a freezer this huge?" He opened it up and saw that it was still working despite the power being off. "I read in the paperwork that I was sent that the kitchen is on its own line. A direct feed, though I haven't any idea what that means."

"There is a grid on the property that was put in when the electric company was formed. The contract with the company says that so long as the house is here and they allow the company to maintain a clear path to the substation, then they will get free power." Evan asked Joshua why the entire house wasn't powered by it. "Not sure, but I'm thinking that this part of the house was all that was here when the company was formed. You should be able to hook the rest of the house up to it without any trouble."

"Free electric. That's wonderful." They looked over the rest of the house on the lower level. Dylan sat down on the fireplace skirt in the dining room and he went to sit next to her. "How are you feeling?"

"Pretty good, actually. I tire easily, but I'm feeling better." He wondered if he should tell her why and decided that he'd wait until they were alone. She might want to hurt him, and he wasn't sure that he wouldn't let her. It was sexy when she got all huffy with him. "I think that we need to talk about the expense of renovating this house. I have some money, but not a great deal. I get a check from the government once a month, so you could take that to do some of the repairs."

"We have money." She shook her head. "We do, I told you that. The fact that this house needs work is all right. We can do things with it that we might not have had it been in perfect shape. Not to mention, we both got a good deal on it because it needs work. And before we know it, it'll be all done."

"It's a lot of money." He said he knew that. "I mean, the kitchen alone could be upwards of ten grand. That's just for one room. This place has nine bedrooms, four and a half baths, not counting the master suite, as well as others we need. Getting a good deal on the house isn't going to be that helpful if you have to spend more on the repairs than you paid for it."

"Do you like this house? I do. Very much so. I can see having family over in it. There is a nice sized barn out back that I can have a few horses in from my parents' ranch. The banister alone will be great fun for any children we bring into our lives. I remember sliding down my grandparents' when I was little." She told him again it was a lot of money. "Yes, it is. A good deal more than I thought it would be, but Joshua said it was a solid foundation. There weren't any leaks to the roof, and structurally, it's very sound. I think we'll be happy here, once we get it renovated."

"I love this house. Ever since I was a child, I always wanted to live here." He told her that it was settled then. "Where will we live until it's done? I mean, it'll take a long time to get it finished enough for us to even live in."

It was the first time she'd said *us*. He was so happy that he nearly missed what Joshua was saying. When he looked at him, he laughed and repeated it.

"The former owners left you something. I think, anyway. Come into the living room." He was almost afraid to. Evan was happy right now, and the thought of messing it up with something bad…well, he wasn't sure he wanted to see whatever it was. When they entered the room, Joshua was on the phone in the corner.

The boxes were stacked on a large trunk. He asked Dylan if she'd put them there, and she said she'd never been here. Going to the first box, he looked at Joshua when he closed his phone. There was enough dust on the top boxes that he was sure they could plant a garden.

"I just talked to the realtor. He said that the house was bought as is. Whatever we find, it's part of the house. But he said if you find a body, he never wants to know about it." Evan asked him if he told them about this. "I did, and he just kept saying, as is. I think they're just glad to have it off their books again. And I talked to Adrian, and he said that you should open it and toss it if you don't want it. That's my advice too. But, I must go. Dad is wanting to get a piece of furniture moved out of the barn, and he wants me to bring it here. I guess you'll have furniture when you move in."

"Mom said she had a lot of things in storage…some of it was

our relatives'. For now, I guess we'll store things in the barn as we come across them." Joshua said that was an excellent idea.

When Joshua was gone, taking Grandda with him, Evan looked at Dylan. "You ready to see what we have here?"

"I don't know. What if it's one of the previous owners that has been cut up and stuffed in the trunk? His other parts are in the boxes." Evan laughed and said it wasn't. "But how do you know?"

"I don't smell death." Dylan looked at the box, then at him. "I can smell better than humans. I don't smell death in this house at all. And so you know, me being a cat, we'll never have to worry about mice or any other vermin coming in to roost either. They'll be afraid of me."

She laughed. It was a good sound, one that he thought he could hear every day and it still would not be enough. Pulling the first box off the top of the pile of about a dozen, he set it on the floor and realized he had nothing to open it with. Dylan handed him a knife that she took from her boot. Having her around, he thought, was going to be handy. Kissing her quickly, he punched the knife into the box and tore the tape away.

"Oh my."

Chapter 7

Dylan walked the plank. It really wasn't a plank, but a steady bar that she used to hang onto while learning to use her broken body again. It was easier today. Even much easier than it had been just two days ago. Not only was she able to walk without holding on, but she didn't have to rest as much either. It was as if she was regaining every part of her body back. Pausing at the end to think about that, she turned to look at her mom when she came into the room.

"You're doing well, darling. I'm so happy." She nodded and carefully made her way back to the end of the bars. "I was hoping that I could persuade you to have lunch with me. Well, me and Eve. She's meeting me at the restaurant near the mall in about an hour."

"Mom, she likes you." Mom nodded and sat down as Dylan made her way to the end again. "Evan asked me to refer to myself as Dylan; did you know that?"

"I'm so glad. Everyone calling you Hutch made me think of large pieces of furniture from the twenties. Whatever do I have to do for that man for convincing you of that?" Dylan laughed. "I know that Eve likes me. She's told me several times. But it's

93

so difficult, if you want to know the truth. I find myself wanting to ask her if I should wait on her or something."

"She's really nice. Did I tell you that she's going through the furniture in their storage unit and giving us what she no longer needs? It's kind of nice, having so much furniture that I don't know what to do with it." Her mom told her that she'd been living in the wild for too long. "No kidding. Oh, before I forget again, we might have a few pieces to send your way if you want them. Adam bought his grandda's house, and said he has too much for him. I think he likes the more modern things rather than the antiques in the house."

"I'd love that. If you're sure you don't want it." She assured her mom that she'd taken what she wanted. "Your dad is going to work with Oliver. He's never done that sort of work before, working on a ranch, but Oliver said it was easy work for the most part. Even your grandda is going to go out with them. I think he's doing this because we're poor."

"Perhaps. But that's not such a bad thing, is it? I don't mean the poor part, but the working. And you're not poor so long as I have a job and money." Her mom said she didn't want people to feel sorry for them. "I doubt that any of them would feel sorry for us. I mean, they're a really nice bunch of people. I like them. Don't you?"

"I do. They've welcomed us with open arms, and have done so much for us. Grandda has someone with him a few hours a day so that your dad and I can do things. Mostly it's just to go to the store or the library, but it's nice, just to be by ourselves for a little while. We were thinking about having dinner out and a movie soon. We've not done that in years." Dylan told her she looked happier too. "Oh, I didn't mean for you to think that I wasn't happy."

"I didn't, Mom. I'm only saying that you look happy. Grandda is a lot for anyone. But you and Dad, you need a break too. I'm glad that you're getting it." Mom nodded and watched her walk the bars. "I have to do this for twenty minutes a day. I'm nearly done now. I can't believe how much better I'm feeling."

"It's the tiger." Dylan asked her what she meant. "I read this story once...it was one of those books you don't read, the smutty kind, where when a shifter exchanges blood with a human, who takes on some of the tiger's traits. Like healing. I never believed it until you started living with Evan."

Dylan nearly stumbled. "You mean, this is because of Evan? Do you think...? Well, of course he knows it. I wonder why.... He thought I'd freak out, so he didn't say anything to me. I wonder if he would have eventually."

"More than likely. And by freaking out, you mean like you are now?" She was too. Her heartrate was really high and she felt slightly dizzy. Blood, his blood, had healed her more than she'd ever thought. "Dylan, calm down. I might be wrong."

"You're not." As she made her way to the end of the bars again, she stopped. Moving to the chair next to her mom, she sat there and felt.... Well, it was like someone was touching her mind. Then Evan spoke to her.

Are you all right? She didn't know what to say, much less answer him. *Honey, are you all right?*

"I don't... how are you doing this?" He laughed and she wanted to punch him. "Evan, I don't think this is funny. How are you talking to me?"

I can hear your thoughts. Just think of talking to me and you

95

won't have to speak aloud. That freaks people out and they think that you're nuts. She asked him where he was. *My office, currently. I have to go and check on two patients in about a half hour. Where are you?*

In the rehabilitation lab. My mom is here with me. She came to invite me to lunch with her and your mom. He told her that was good. *I'm healing. Did you know that?*

Yes. I was going to talk to you about it when we got back to my parents' last night, but you distracted me again. I love having you suck my cock. Her body warmed when she thought of all the things they'd done to each other last night. *I'd like to wake you that way in the morning. My cat would as well.*

I can't talk to you about that right now. I told you, my mom is here. Evan laughed again. *Damn it. I don't know why I love you.*

There was silence. It was profound too, like an open line on a phone. When he did speak again, she was almost afraid to answer him. He sounded so...sexy.

Do you love me? She told him she thought so. *I'm so glad to hear that. I'll have to work harder on making you sure that you love me. You should know that I love you with all that I am, Dylan. And I want you to be my wife as soon as we can arrange it.*

Can we...? *I can't talk to you about this way. This is more of a face to face sort of thing.* Evan laughed then asked her about the house. *Mom and I were going to go see it today, if I could convince her that I want her to. She thinks the oddest things at times. She's afraid of intruding on my life, when all I want her to do is be a big part of it. I've missed having her around me all the time. Someone that I can talk to. I love my family.*

Mine too. I think they're worried about each other too. My mom is worried that yours doesn't like her, and Dad is afraid of stepping on toes *when he talks to Norris. They have to get over this.* Dylan told him what his mom had said. *I know. My mom said that your mom was so tense when they were together. I think you having lunch with them might break that up. Mom really likes Stella.*

And my mom does her as well. If she could ever get over this upper-class verses lower-class thing. It's making her a little standoffish, I think. Evan said they'd get better at it. *Is the house being worked on?*

Yes. There are two crews there today. One of them is doing the rewiring and hooking up the house on the main station like the kitchen is already, and the other is gutting the kitchen. The old wood is going to be made into something for the house. Dad and Grandpa are working on it. She wondered what it would be. *Don't know. But my grandpa is good with wood working. He did it as a younger man. I think he's as excited as he's ever been about something.*

When she was finished taking a shower and dressed, she met her mom and Eve in the main lobby. Evan was with them. When he kissed her like he'd not seen her in days instead of a few hours, she felt embarrassed again. Dylan supposed she'd have to get used to the way he liked to hug and be hugged.

"I was just telling the ladies here that when you go to the house, I'd like for them to help you with the tile for the floor. There are some samples there, but if you don't like them, we can go look in the store tomorrow." She asked him for what room. "The kitchen and the pantry. I was also thinking hardwoods in the dining room and the main hall. The rest we'll work on as we go."

When she was helped into the car, he leaned in and kissed her again. "I don't know a thing about picking out tile. What if I get it all wrong?" He kissed her again. "Evan, that's not helping

97

me."

"Sure, it is, or at least it's helping me. But I'm sure you'll do fine. And so you know, the samples that are there are ones that my dad picked out. So, don't be surprised if you don't like them." She asked him why not. "He has a very eclectic taste when it comes to putting things together."

When he left them to go back into the building, she looked at her mom and future mother-in-law. She wasn't sure what to say to them about the tile they were to see to after lunch. If Oliver picked them out, shouldn't she like at least one of them? But instead of saying anything, she told them about what was going on with the house. And there was a lot.

"The roof is sound, but they're going over it today to make sure that there are no leaks." Her mom asked when they'd be ready to move in. "Evan says in about a month. I don't see that happening. The kitchen is being gutted, the bathrooms on all the floors are having the same thing done to them, and they're enlarging some of the rooms. There is the smallest bathroom you've ever seen in the hall upstairs. The plumbing is being replaced as they work; it's in good shape, but if we're going to do it, we might as well make sure we don't have to cut back into this anytime soon. I don't see us moving in that quickly, do you?"

"You'd be surprised. If Evan says a month, I'm betting that it'll be less. He'll hire as many firms as it takes to get it done, and pay to have them working overtime." That was a lot of money, Dylan thought. All this construction was going to be enough as it was without him making them work a lot of overtime. "Honey, don't worry about it. You'll have a lovely house soon, and then you can start hosting parties."

"Parties? I don't know how to have a party. I don't think I've even been to one in a decade." Dylan looked at her mom. "You know anything about this?"

"No, but I'm sure you'll do well. You're very determined, and whatever you decide to do, it'll be perfect." Sure, when it came to doing her job, but a party? No way in hell was she able to do that. "Dylan, we're going to be at the restaurant soon. Are you all right?"

"Yes. I'm all right." She wasn't, and she was sure that her mom knew it. "Where are we going, anyway? I forgot to ask."

"There is this really nice little bistro by the mall. I've eaten there a few times with Oliver and we really had a nice time. I thought we'd get a table in the corner and go over your plans for the house. If not, then I'm sure we can find a great deal more to talk about." Dylan nodded. "Evan said you were trying to find yourself a job. Did you have anything in mind?"

"Yes. I talked to someone on the police force this morning, and I was going to teach gun safety classes. Mostly to adults, but to kids that are curious about it as well." Her mom said that was splendid. "And Randy called me last night asking me to help him with a couple of projects as well. Nothing that I'd have to travel to do, but some work for the government. His boss...well, *our* boss, is coming to talk to me soon. I don't think that'll be a big deal either. He's more than likely glad to be rid of me. I've been a pain in the ass for some time, I think."

"You'd do well at both those jobs, I think. You've had a great deal more training on the gun safety than most on the police, I would imagine." She told Eve that was what the captain there had said. "I know Mark Fleming. He's a good man to work with. You'll do him a great service with the gun safety, I think."

"Yes. He seems to think we could get into a few classrooms at the school, and that'll help at hunting season." Eve said she'd make a few calls. "Mark said you'd do that as well. He told me that you could get it done faster than he could."

"I know a few people." Dylan laughed. "And here we are. Let's enjoy the food and have some fun, shall we? Oh, and Stella, I have something I'd like to talk to you about. How would you like to become a member of the Monthly Readers? It's a group of us that gets together once a month to talk about something that we're reading. Usually we have too much fun to ever get around to actually talking about the books, but the food is good and so is the company."

By the time they were finished eating, her mom was much more relaxed and seemed to be enjoying herself. Dylan got a few more answers about what was going on about her healing, as well as ideas about the house. When they pulled up in front of her new home, she wasn't the least bit surprised to not only see several vans with different logos on them, but also Oliver and Ollie. Her dad was helping too, but mostly watching over Grandda. And they looked like they were having a blast.

~~~

Evan walked the shell that had once been the kitchen. Walls had been knocked out, windows too, but they were being replaced today. Shelving was being put in the pantry, and the freezer was being cleaned out. A lot of work had been done since he'd been here two days ago. He looked at his dad when he joined him in the room.

"You should see that mate of yours. She's in there telling them men what she wants like she's done this before." Evan told him about the tile. "She's right, you know. Having the

100

floor all torn up, it only makes sense to have heat put down in here. This room will be something that you spend a lot of time in, and it might as well be comfy."

"She picked the tile that you liked too." Dad nodded and smiled. "I think once this room is finished, she'll feel better about the money being spent, don't you?"

"Nope. I think she's gonna worry on money all your life. And that's not a bad thing either. Just because there is a lot of it doesn't mean that you shouldn't be careful of it. I love the girl." Evan told him he did as well. "I know it, son. It's all over your face. And I like the things she has in mind for this place too. I never would have thought of some of the things she's having done."

She'd had a lot of great ideas, and ways to make them less expensive as well. Like the old quartz countertops in the kitchen were being cut down to put in the downstairs bathroom. The beautiful marble that had been used around the fireplace in the living room had been carefully removed and sent to be cleaned. It would be replaced in a few days and look fantastic.

There were great changes going on too. He'd spoken with one of the men on the construction company, and he'd shown him what she'd suggested. Making the nine bedrooms on the upper floors into five. Putting in larger closets, as well as enlarging the bathrooms. Carpets in the rooms had been taken up, and oak flooring had been discovered. They were going to sand those down and use those instead of carpets.

"She's not touched the master, so you know." He asked his dad why not. "Don't know, other than she hasn't even answered any of the questions asked about the area. I think she's waiting on you to help her. Could be wrong, but I don't think so."

"All right. I'll talk to her after she's done in the office. Did she mention the boxes and trunks that we were left?" His dad said he didn't know anything about them. "They were full of money. I mean millions of dollars' worth of cash. I have someone working with Joshua to see if it's from a bank robbery or something. There were also some jewels, as well as a few thousand shares in a few companies. We're talking a lot more money than should have been just sitting around an abandoned house."

"Woo wee. That's great for the both of you. I'm guessing that you're keeping it to yourself until you find out who it might belong to." Evan told his dad what the bank had said. "Even after you figure it out, I'd keep it on the lowdown. Some people might have a bit to say about it, and it won't be good. Just use it for something good. Like helping out her parents or something like that. They sure could use it."

"I was thinking the same thing. They've been struggling for some time now. I guess he was let go when one of the plants closed up a few years back. But the bank sent over a document that we both signed that said the house was being bought by us as is, and that any contents real or expected were ours as well. Joshua said they just wanted it off their books. It had been foreclosed on about twenty years ago when the woman who owned it passed away." His dad said he remembered that. "Did you know the family that lived here? Maybe they want it back."

"No. They're all dead, so far as I know. There was a man and a woman, if I remember correctly, but I don't think they were married. Quite a scandal back then. Women didn't live with men without marriage. I think he had some kids, or she did. Can't remember that much, but it was something. But it's been years, like you said. Nobody has lived here in some time; I think it's been longer than twenty years." His dad looked around the house as he continued. "I never talked to them much, the McFarlands…or it could have been Decker. Like I said, it's been a long time. They were nice enough, I suppose. Kept to themselves a great deal. The mister, he was a nice man. The woman, she was a hellion, I heard, all the way up until she passed. Your momma, she never cared for her. If there were kids, which I do remember some younger ones running around, they're long since dead too."

"You think this money, it's just been here waiting on someone to come and claim it? It's odd, don't you think, that it was piled up in the living room like it was?" His dad nodded but didn't say anything. "Dad, why do I have the feeling you might know something?"

"There was some speculation that the mister — I can't rightly remember his first name right now — but it was thought that he deferred to her whenever things were brought up. Timid, I think you'd call him. When he passed away, she took it hard. The town suffered too, I guess. She had her hand in about everything. Then she sort of snapped out of it and started helping some more. She's responsible for the library that we have. A few other buildings too that are now closed down. Anyway, they said that she roamed this house, just wandered around it, waiting for her one true love. I don't know most of it, but you have to wonder now, don't you?" Evan asked if he believed that. "Don't know, son. I mean, I suppose she could have been brokenhearted about him dying. I know that I would be. But back then, I never really gave it much in the way of time to think on. But you and Dylan, you'll make it your home now.

Give it life again with children and family. I'm thinking that if she left the money for the next family, then you should make sure that you do this house up right and have a wonderful life in it."

"But the money...why leave it in the living room like it was?" Dad said he didn't know, but not to go looking for trouble until he found out about it. Evan thought it was good advice, but a little hard to do. Found money was nice when you pulled jeans out of the dryer, but this was too much to just think you could afford to take a little trip with.

Evan went in search of Dylan. She was in the dining room just off the kitchen, staring at the wall. He came up behind her and wrapped his arms around her, and she leaned back into him. Evan thought he could stand this way for a very long time.

"I think we need a window here." He looked at the wall and tried to think what was on the other side of it that they'd look at while in this room. "There is a garden just outside here that needs some work, as well as a barn that looks to be as old as the house. Not the big one in back, but this one is like a milk house."

"Let's have a look." They made their way around the construction crew and their equipment to go out onto the deck that surrounded the house. "It looks like it might have been a rose garden at one time. See the little blooms? And I think that's hydrangeas too. This would be something spectacular to look at in the spring and summer months. And if that is a milk house, there would be a nice stream under it to keep the horses happy if we get any."

"Your mom and mine said that it was a show garden. I don't know what that means, but they seemed to think that there was a trellis here, as well as flowers growing up it. I'd like to put that back someday." He thought that was an excellent idea. "Your brother, Blake, he came by a little while ago and said that he'd take care of it. He likes to work with the soil and wants to bring this garden back. I hope you don't mind, but I told him to go for it."

"I'm glad. And he is good with plants. He has a nice garden at the house that the cook uses. I think he does it so that he can relax. Blake loves ranching and all that goes with it, but he loves the ground too." He looked around the yard that was mostly overgrown. "It's sad that it got this bad. Mom said that there was an iron fence that went all around the house and gardens."

She didn't say anything but did sit on the swing that was still hanging. He didn't sit, afraid that as old as it was, it might not hold them both. When Dylan started to make the thing creak with each rock, he sat on the floor and waited.

"I have a few contacts in high places. I want to tell you that so that when I go away, you'll know that I'm telling you the truth as to what I'm up to. He's here, to talk to us both. Mostly you, but he wants to have a conversation with both of us before he leaves again." He said that he'd believe her even if she was telling him that she was talking about the president. She just looked at him.

"You know him?" She nodded. "I see. And he is...I'm not even sure what I should say now. I mean, I believe you, but.... You know the president?"

"Yes. I know him well. I've been working directly with him for a long time. Randy reports to him, and I do as well. We're...I guess you could say that I'm his go to man when he needs something done." Evan nodded. "I talked to him today,

105

this afternoon. A phone was delivered to me here about an hour ago. I took the call as soon as I turned it on. It's about the money."

"He's telling you that it's from a robbery? That it's not ours." She shook her head. "But we can't keep it."

"Yes, it's ours. And anything else that we find in the house. He's pulled a few strings and made sure that no one can come back on us about it either." Evan nodded, then something occurred to him. "I can see your mind working, and he does have a favor to ask of us. You mostly, but he said it would not have a thing to do with the money if you were to say no."

"What is it? I'm not saying that I'll agree, but I don't want him to blackmail us should this turn out to be something that I don't want." She looked to her right and he did too. "Holy fuck."

"Yes, she said that you'd not be happy with things." The president sat down on the chair that someone placed behind him. "Do have a nicer seat, Evan. I'd hate to strain my neck to have a conversation with you. And I do need to speak to you both."

CHAPTER 8

Dylan was still on the swing waiting for Henry and Evan to return. They'd gone to the barn to talk, and she'd been just too tired to go with them because she'd been up since dawn and had been going since. She was still swinging when her grandda joined her. It was getting close to supper time, she knew, so he'd be a little more lost than usual.

"I was looking for my Dylan." She patted the seat next to her and he stood staring at her. "Do I know you?"

"I'm Dylan, your granddaughter. How you doing, Grandda? You like the house?" He looked at the door he'd just come out of and then back at her. "Come and swing with me. We'll enjoy the evening air a little before going home."

He sat, but he didn't seem to be enjoying it. She slowed her rocking down enough that he could relax. Her grandda had been the world to her when growing up. Grandma too. Dylan missed them both so much. This disease that he had, it was slowly hurting them all, she thought.

"I'm confused." She told him that was all right. She'd help him. "There is a man in there that I don't know, but he calls me Ollie. He said he's Evan's dad. I don't know who Evan is either, but I didn't know how to say that."

"Evan is the man I'm going to be married to soon. His dad's name is Oliver. If you spoke to Ollie, that would be Mr. Whitfield's father. Evan's grandda." He nodded, but still looked like he wasn't sure. "Grandda, did you see all the renovations going on in the house? Grandma said you loved to do that sort of thing when you were younger."

"I miss her so much." Dylan told him she did as well. "The house is nice. Did you know that there was a family living here? They were the McFarlands. I think they're dead now."

"They are. Mr. Decker, we think his name was, died first, then she followed sometime later." He nodded and started to swing a little harder. "Mom said that you're doing well with the therapy. Do you like it?"

"I don't know." She let it go, and decided that they'd talk of things he'd bring up so as not to upset him. "I would like to go and get an ice cream later. I love the kind with nuts on it. I used to share one with my Dylan."

"We can do that. After we have some pizza. I thought we'd all go there after we leave here and have some. You like pizza?" He said that he did, but just plain. "Yes. Me too. Sometimes I like it with the works, but cheese pizza is the best. Like vanilla ice cream."

They moved the swing back and forth, and Dylan decided that she was going to have this one redone or replaced so that she could enjoy this kind of time with her grandda. When her dad came out of the house and sat on the president's chair, she smiled at him.

"I'm going to be working for Oliver on his ranch, did your mom tell you?" She said that she had and asked if he was excited. "Yes. I know little to nothing about horses or cattle, but I'm excited to be doing something rather than being at home. Dad is going to be joining me too when he wants to."

Her dad had been a teacher when she was a child. But the school that he'd taught in had been closed when a bunch of children and teachers had been murdered one day. Her dad had been able to save a lot of children with his quick thinking, and she thought it sad that he'd been asked to step down...too many memories for the students when the new school opened. He'd been retired with full pay, but it wasn't the same for him after that. He had worked for one of the manufacturing plants for a while after that, but it too had closed down and he'd lost his job again.

"I'm sure you'll do fine. Evan and his brothers spend a lot of time there as well." Dad nodded. "What is it you're going to be doing, do you know yet?"

"I'm going to be learning how to drive the tractor first. I've so wanted to do that. Then we'll see what I can do after that. I guess they grow a lot of straw and wheat for the local farmers." She had heard that as well. "Your mom is having fun with Eve. I guess you guys had a nice lunch too."

"Yes, we did." Grandda stood up and so did her dad. She looked to where they were looking and smiled. They were going to meet Henry, it seemed. "Dad, Grandda, I'd like for you both to meet Henry Cobb. Henry, this is Norris, my dad, and Bailey, my grandda."

"You're the president." Henry nodded and said that he was. "I mean, you're here. In my daughter's house, and you're the president. Are we in...? Did we do something wrong?"

"No, not at all, but your daughter has been doing me some

favors, and when I found out that she had herself a man in her life as well as a lovely new home, I thought I'd come and see it for myself." They all sat when Henry told them to. "You've a wonderful daughter here, Mr. Hutchinson. She's done this country proud."

"I'm very proud of her myself. She's gone through hell and come back to us." Henry nodded and smiled. "She works for you? I mean, you said she's done you some favors. So, she reports to you?"

"She does and will continue to do so. I was just talking to her husband-to-be. Evan has agreed to help me out as well. He was just showing me the barn. It's quite a nice piece of property here, don't you think?" Dad nodded and looked at her. "Yes, sir. A very fine daughter you have."

"You know him." She laughed and said that she did. "You never said...well I guess you'd not be able to tell us who you were working for. My goodness, Dylan, you work for the president, and he's here."

"Yes, Dad, he's here, and he's a very nice man." The rest of the family came out then, and she wondered if Evan had asked them to. As introductions were made, she watched each of their faces. This might have been funny had it not been so serious. "He needs for us to travel with him for the next few days. While we're gone, Henry is going to have someone stay here and oversee the house. It'll need some updates that can't be done by the local companies."

Evan continued to explain when she looked at him. "Dylan has been working for Henry the president, for some years, and he'd like for her to continue to do so. He's come here to assure me that she'll be as safe as he can make her, and that so will you all."

"Should we be worried?" Dylan told her mom that there wasn't anything to worry about. "You mean, for us to worry about or for you to worry about? I don't want you hurt again, Dylan. You're my child."

"I'll be fine, Mom. I promise. I'm not going to leave the country again." Dylan glanced at Henry, then continued to reassure her mom. "I'm going to do some work with him on a low-profile level. Mostly to help with his team, as well as some development of plans. Evan will go with me when he can, but for the most part, I'm going to fly there and back in a single day. There will be times when I'll have to stay longer, but I'll always let you know when I do."

"You have known about this for some time, I take it." Eve looked at her, then at Evan. "You knew about this?"

"Not until she did. He contacted her today. Are you mad, Mom?" She said that she wasn't, but was afraid for them both. "I am as well, but he needs her as much as we do. I don't want anything to happen to her either, but this is important. Not just for us, but for the country as a whole. She's that important to him."

"I understand that. I do. But you're my boy and I don't want you to be injured, nor Dylan. I need you both." Evan hugged his mom and she wiped at the tears. Looking at Henry, Dylan nearly laughed when he took a step back from her. "I'm holding you responsible for my children. You let them get hurt and I will hunt you down and rip your throat out of you. That is not an idle threat, either. They get hurt and there will never be a place you can go where I won't find you."

"Perhaps, my dear lady, I hired the wrong Whitfield." He

kissed Eve's hand and smiled at her. "Nothing will happen to either of them, I will make it my only priority when they're with me to keep them as safe as I would my own family."

"You'd better." Eve hugged Evan again and suggested that they go back to their home and have dinner. "You're welcome to join us, sir. We're having steaks on the grill and baked potatoes. Homemade ice cream too."

"As good as that sounds, I have to get back. There are few that know I'm here, so if you could, I'd very much appreciate it if you'd keep my visit to yourselves." Everyone agreed, including her grandda. "Thank you all so very much. And again, thank you for letting me borrow Hutch for a little while longer."

After he was gone, they each loaded up in their cars. Dylan was waiting until they were gone before she left with Evan. As soon as the last car was out of sight, she turned to him and let him hold her.

"Are you all right with this?" He said that he was more than all right with it. "I'm so glad. When he called me, I wasn't sure I even wanted to work for him, but I knew that I'd not be making any decision until you were briefed. It'll mean a lot of travel for us. Especially for me."

"So long as you call me when you're there and on your way back to me, we'll be fine." She told him that she loved him. "And I love you as well. But he did suggest that we marry, and soon. How are you about that?"

"Great. I think it's an excellent idea." She was surprised when he went down on one knee in front of her. "Evan, what are you doing?"

"Asking you properly. Now hush, I want this to be perfect." He pulled out a ring and put it on her finger. It was beautiful.

"Dylan Hutchinson, will you be my wife? Forever? Will you love me no matter how many times I have to leave you in the middle of the night? Keep me safe and yourself safe for me? Will you take me into your life for all time, and love me as much as I do you?"

"I will." He stood up then and kissed her. It was deep and full of heat. And when he lifted his head, telling her not to run, she stepped back against the house when he changed into a large tiger.

~~~

Evan knew that she was afraid of him. He sat as still as he could while she stared at him. He didn't speak to her either, fearful that she would take off. Dylan seemed to be right on the edge of freaking out.

"You're beautiful. I'm not sure handsome applies right now, but you are handsome." His cat purred at her. "I'm assuming that you've been wanting to show me him for a few days now."

Yes. He's very anxious to meet you. He also wants to mark you as his as well. She asked how that would work. *He bites you. It'll hurt, but not for very long. It's something that tigers do, I guess.*

"You guess? You mean you don't have any idea why he wants to bite me?" Evan told Dylan that the cat loved her. "Oh. I guess that's the way it should be since you do. And why did you ask me not to run?"

He'll chase you. Maybe knock you down. He would never hurt you on purpose, but he's a lot bigger than you are and it might hurt. She said she wasn't at the running point yet anyway. *There is that too. He wants to drink from you as well.*

"What does that mean, exactly?" He laughed in her head. "I'm sorry you find me to be such a novice at this, but I'm not

113

having sex with that monster."

He knocked her back to the wall, then to the floor. He was careful of her, as he didn't want to hurt her. But when she was under his cat, Evan could feel the purr all the way to his feet. Instead of being upset, as he fully expected her to be, she put her hands in the fur around his face and held him.

"You're scary big, did you know that?" He nodded. "I love you, Evan, but I'm a little afraid of this creature that you can be. Not terrified, but afraid of his size, his teeth, and how strong he is."

He'd never harm you. In fact, we'd give our life to keep you safe and out of harm's way. Telling his cat to be careful of their mate, he moved down her body. She wasn't shaking, but he knew she was afraid. Her scent was calling to them both to be extra careful. *He wants you to pull your pants off for him. Me too, but he can go first.*

She hesitated a moment or two too long for his cat, and he clawed at her pants. Evan heard her laughing as she pushed his paws out of the way and sat up. There was something so incredibly sexy about her sitting there all mussed up.

"He's more impatient than you are, I think. Christ, I must be insane for doing this." Her pants were off, as well as her panties. When she grabbed his fur again it was painful, and his cat snarled. The smack to his nose had him whimpering. "You hurt me, touch me in any way that's not just oral, and I will kill you. Understand?"

He felt the fear of her run over his cat. And when he nodded, without the encouragement of Evan, he had to laugh himself. His cat was terrified of his mate.

She was spread out before them and Evan was slightly

afraid for himself. He'd made love to her, yes, but this was different. This seemed more carnal to him. And when his cat made his way up her leg, tasting her skin, nipping at her flesh, Evan didn't even have to warn him to be extra careful, to go slowly this first time.

He licked her from gate to clit. When she cried out, he was sure that he'd hurt her somehow and looked at her. She was bowed up from the floor, her face tight with her release. And when he licked her again, taking her hard clit into his large mouth, Dylan screamed so loudly that Evan was sure that she was going to be hoarse in the morning.

His cat enjoyed her. Dylan came several more times, each time flooding his mouth with cream. And when she begged him to stop, to let her breathe, he did so easily and let Evan take his body back. He buried his mouth over her pussy and devoured her.

"Please. Oh please, I need a minute." Evan wasn't ready to stop, and didn't until she pulled his head up. "You're killing me. I can't.... Not anymore. Please, you have to stop."

He moved up her body, kissing and tasting every part of her until he reached her breasts. Taking them into his mouth one at a time, Evan suckled at her nipples, took as much of her flesh into his mouth as he could before biting her. When Dylan wrapped her legs around his hips, he slid into her heat, made easier by how wet she was.

"Take me." He moaned at her command, unable to put into words how much he needed her, how very much he loved her. Filling her over and over, making his body hum with the need to mark her, Evan nearly came when she offered him her throat.

The bite was harder than he'd meant. She cried out, then

held him to her as she continued to come. When he felt his own climax race over himself, Evan's cat took just enough of him to bite her harder in the shoulder.

She screamed out his name but never let him go. Even as he filled her, his body pounding her as hard as he could, she held him. When Evan was complete, his body aching from the storm that seemed to have taken him, he dropped atop her and tried to catch his breath.

"You killed me. Or pretty close." He laughed and looked down at her. "You're very good at this, did anyone ever...you know what? Don't answer that. I don't think I would like the answer."

"You make me want to be a better man." Evan rolled to his back and took her with him so that she was on top this time. "I don't think we're going to make dinner with the family. And we might, just maybe, miss breakfast as well."

"Good. I needed some time with you alone." She laid her head on his chest and he held her. Her skin was so soft, her body limp with exhaustion. He thought she'd fallen asleep until she started talking softly. "Henry said that you are going to help him find a physician. I thought he'd ask you to be it."

"I was asked, but I turned him down. I would have to live in DC all the time, and I don't think I'd like that anymore than you would." She looked at him, resting her head on her fist. "He was very nice about it, telling me that if I ever changed my mind I'd be welcome, but I like what I do here. Being a surgeon is all I ever wanted."

"No, I don't think I'd want to live in a big city. I love this little town." She laid back down. "When I work, there will be times when you can't make it, I understand that. But Henry said that I could, for the most part, work from here. I'll have to have a bigger office. Also, secure lines coming in and going out. They'll have someone checking our home periodically, as well as cars that we might purchase and use. Your family's as well."

"I figured as much. And you'll need it. I think he was planning on having the barn converted into an office sort of place for you. He seems to think that no one will think of it as anything more than that, a big barn." Evan thought of what else they had discussed, and thought about bringing it up now. "He said that my family would be protected at all costs. I asked him what that meant. He said that we'd have security on the property, and that each person that we encounter on a regular basis would have to be vetted. It took me a few minutes to figure that one out. I don't care for all that. I understand the necessity of it, but I don't care for it."

"I know. My family as well. My grandda, he's going to need more care than we can provide for him when things start to go forward. I mean, he can't be trusted with a lot of the things going on, not with his mind so confused all the time." Evan knew that as well. "When I start working, will you go with me the first few times? I mean, if you can? We'll have a home in DC too…he doesn't think it'll be easy to keep us under wraps if we're in a hotel all the time. So he's going to look into purchasing a home for us so that we'll feel less like we're on display and more homey."

"Yes. We'll look for something when he's ready." She thanked him. "He told me some of the things that he's going to be having you do. But to be honest, I think he was giving me the civilian information instead of the husband to the employee version."

117

"I would say so. But what I'm going to be doing is covert things. Not out in the field, I can't do that anymore. I'll be working with people that will be going out on missions. Showing them how to blend in. I know a few languages as well, and I'll be teaching them some of the more useful words. Also, how to read a map." He asked her what that meant. "In the classes we took before we were put out to work, there was a class on how to make GPS work for us. Also a compass. But that shit means nothing when you're in the middle of a war zone and most of the things, like street signs, are gone. So, having some sort of map, any part of it, can go a long way into figuring out where you are."

He'd never thought of that. And he rarely used a map for anything anymore, not with his trusty GPS on his phone. She explained to him that the use of phones would get them killed. Tracking and the lights would be a perfect way to blow cover. Not to mention any sort of noises. Also, she mentioned that anything on a phone, should it be lost, could get family killed as well. She was going to be teaching that to men and woman that might not think of all the troubles that could go with it.

As they got up to get dressed—lucky for him he had a bag in the car for them both now—he asked her about some of the other things she'd been trained to do. There was a great deal more than he'd imagined.

"How to know what we can eat and drink and not. There are canned foods everywhere if you know where to look. Knowing a grocery store in their language. There are also things of the earth that can be eaten, but some also can easily kill you." Again, things he would never have thought of. "Sometimes the enemy will put out a fake grocery store. The shelves will be filled with canned goods that have been tampered with. It happens a lot more than you would think. I can train them to know what to look for so that no one dies from that. A great deal more too."

"So, you're going to be the person that is giving them all the smaller ins and outs of working in country that they can't learn in a classroom." She nodded and sat on the floor while he finished dressing. "You know, that's sort of scary when you think of the lengths that people go to in order to win a war."

"Yes, but you do know that we do no less than that." He nodded and told her that he figured that too. "You're okay with this? Me working for the government?"

"Of course I am. They need you as much as I do, but in a different way. You're saving them from themselves. I mean, with you there giving them a heads up on things, it might make my job a little easier here. Some of the men who come back, they're not well. And I don't mean with just the injuries that they might incur while there."

They were driving to his parents' house when he remembered a few more things that Henry had told him. Pay for one. They'd be paid in cash so no one would be able to trace checks back to the source. Also, life and health insurance would be paid for them, as well as any upgrades to their home that was going to keep them safe.

There were more benefits coming their way as well, most of them costly. A car would be provided for them when here and in DC. His insurance would be paid to keep him safe as a doctor. And they'd have a lawyer, their entire family would, to help if anything—and Henry had stressed that word—came up that they might encounter. He wondered now what sort of things he might be anticipating.

CHAPTER 9

Adrian laid the phone back in the cradle and sat back in his chair. He was still trying to wrap his head around the conversation he'd just had when his secretary came into his office and sat across from him. Lily Blair had been with him since he'd opened his doors almost six years ago now.

"Was that really who they said they were?" He nodded. "Do I want to know why the President of the United States is calling here for you?"

"More than likely, but right now I'm trying to put my head back on straight." She snorted at him. "Did you know that I'm pretty smart?"

"No. Are you?" He laughed with her. "Yes, I've told you that from the very beginning. He called you up to tell you that?"

"No. That was what he told me when I told him I'd have to think about the job offer." She cocked a brow at him. "He wants me to run for governor of the state. First, he said that I should run for mayor—and I'd have his vote, he said—then governor. I told him I didn't have the balls for that."

"You'd be very good at both jobs." She smiled at him. "I'm still waiting for you to tell me this was a prank by one of your brothers. Or that grandda of yours. He's a character, by the way."

"He is, but it wasn't any of them. It was Henry Cobb." Lily nodded. "I have to tell you, I'm excited to try this, but.... Well, as I said, I don't think I have the balls for this kind of work. I'm not a very good people person."

"You're not, but you fake it well. And I'd take care of you, if you'd let me." He asked her what she meant. "When you run for mayor, I would work for you if you want."

"Of course I would. Christ, I can't do anything without you." She smiled at him and stood up. "Are we done talking about this?"

"Yes, for now anyway. I'm going to make a few phone calls to get this ball rolling for you." He told her he didn't think he was ready. "You're ready. More than ready. Since you've been a consultant, I've been telling you that you're much too smart to just be the guy behind the ideas. When I think of all the things that you've put into motion for the mayor we have now, without any credit coming your way, I want to pound your head in. You should have gotten credit for those ideas."

"I know. I had no idea when we started working together that he'd be taking all the credit. Like for the play yard for the school. I still think that's what got him elected." Lily said that it was. "Yeah, it's why I've been putting him off about the housing issues."

"You have it all worked out, don't you?" He nodded. "See? You should have been doing this job all along. All your ideas, that'll be your ticket to running things here. And with the support of your family, you'll do wonders."

"I don't think I want them to know." She did that thing that made him think about changing his statement. She would cock her hip out, put her hand on it, and glare. It was almost as scary as his mom's move when she thought he should know better about something. "If I tell even one of them about this, it's going to be a done deal for them. Especially for my grandpa."

"As I said, your grandpa is a hoot. And he'll work so hard to make sure you're elected you might not have to have anyone else in your corner." Adrian told her he had the president. "You do, and that too will help. You'll be a shoo-in for the job."

After she left him, to no doubt tell his family, he thought about the reasons behind Henry wanting him to be mayor. There was a lot of things that he said he could accomplish, but there was also the fact that the current mayor wasn't getting things done.

"The schools have a nice playground, but they're still losing teachers every year. Twelve percent of them only last the first year, and then it jumps to fifty percent that leave after the second. You can't have good teachers if they're leaving before they can make an impact on the lives of children. The clinic downtown is only open one day a week when they should be open every day. People cannot schedule their illnesses that way." He told him that he'd been working on that as well. "I'm sure you have, Adrian, but with the power of the seat behind you, you could actually make a difference."

"I'm just a guy running a firm that helps people make decisions. I mean, I gather the information for them and hand it over. That in no way makes me a good politician." Henry, as he had insisted that he call him, laughed. "Sir, I think you have the wrong Whitfield. My family are ranchers. We raise a few head of cattle, horses, and grow grass and hay. We don't make names for ourselves by running for office."

"I think it's about time that you did. You have a very successful family, Adrian. A brother that is a renowned surgeon. Another that is a worldwide bestselling author. You're a consultant that is asked to help around the world. A rancher that other farmers and ranchers come to when they need help. And not once, that I can find, did you ever turn down anyone that needed it." He asked if he had him checked out. "Of course I did. I can't have my best man with a family that is bad for her. Not that I could have stopped her, as you well know, but I could have taken steps."

"What sort of steps?" No answer. Not that he really expected one, but it did give him a chill to his very core. "Why me? I mean, as you said, there are others that can do this in my family. If you've checked me out, as you said, then you know that I'm not much of a people person."

"Ah, but you are. When pressed, you can talk to people about anything. That is what I need in that seat. A man of all men, and one that can figure out what needs to be done and act upon it." Adrian wasn't sure if that was him or not, but it had felt good to have someone notice something good about him. "You're the perfect man for this job and anything else that you apply for. You are a man who not only gets things going, but asks for help when he needs it."

His family told him he was good all the time, but it had been nice to have a stranger notice. Adrian just wasn't sure what singled him out. Not then, and certainly not now. Getting back to work, he pulled up all he could on the local school system. He was deep into finding the reason that there was such a high turnover when he felt someone in the room with him. Adrian was startled to see his grandpa there.

"Did you find it?" Adrian told him he thought so. "Yeah, you were buried there so deep, I thought I was gonna have to get me a shovel to dig you out again. How about you take an old man to lunch?"

"I don't know any old men." But he stood up and stretched. "I hadn't realized it had gotten so late. This school project was harder than I thought it would be."

"They're losing people all the time there. I was wondering about that myself. You got it under control now?" He said that he knew the reason, or thought he did, but no answer. "You got both and we know it. What is it? Something that can be fixed, or you thinking that it's the people?"

"I can't fix it, but I know someone that can. You're on the board there, aren't you?" He nodded as they got out of the elevator. "You need to fire the current principal at the school. Maybe more, but we'll start with him. I think.... He's doing some underhanded and terrible things, and it's going to get us into trouble when the state comes in."

"What's he doing? Not that I don't believe you, but do I need to bring in the big guns?" Adrian nodded as he got into the car with his grandpa. "That bad, huh? Well, we might as well get it done. But I'm thinking lunch first. I need me some fortification before I tackle something this big."

They ordered and Adrian pulled out the notes that he had written down. "The turnover is high, about thirty-two percent. All women. And I've called a few of them. Grandpa, he's paying these women off." Grandpa looked at him sharply. "It's exactly what is going on in your head right now. Or pretty close. After they've been there a few days, he corners them. When they turn down his sexual advances, he gets them by drugging them then raping them. Each of the women I talked to have had to seek therapy. But, and here's the kicker, he tells them if they say a single word to anyone, he'll ruin them. Most of these women are on a fixed income, with children that they're trying to raise. Good teachers that have gotten hurt by this man. The one woman that I talked to said that she thought herself too old for someone to do those things to."

"Well, that sure does put a different light on things. I want him to serve jail time, not fire him." Adrian said he thought they could do that as well. "You thinking what I'm thinking then? That we do bring in the big guns?"

"Do you mean Dylan?" Grandpa laughed and said that was the ticket. "I was thinking that as well, and I think you're right. She can have one of those talking to Jesus meetings with him."

As they plotted and planned, Evan and Dylan came into the restaurant. Grandpa said he'd called them in, and when they sat down with them, Adrian told them what he'd found out. He looked over at Dylan when she said she'd take care of him.

"He needs to not be dead." She pouted at him and Adrian laughed. "You need to get a confession out of him and then take him in. Mussing him up could get him off to do this again."

"He won't be able to if you let me have my fun." Adrian told her the next time she could. "Okay, but I'm going to hold you to that. A man like him, he needs to be taught a lesson in respect. And I know just how to do it."

They listened to her plan. It was as good, probably better than his. But he was worried about her doing it. When he looked at Evan for some support, he supposed, he shook his head.

She's fine. And I think she needs to feel useful. Adrian said she might get hurt. *I'd be more afraid of Ed getting hurt than her. Every day she gets a lot stronger, and is feeling good. She needs this.*

While he worried, Adrian knew that Evan would never let his mate get hurt. It was not only in their genes to protect their family, but anyone could see that Evan was in love with Dylan and she him. They were, as far as he could see, the perfect match.

~~~

Dylan loved this. She was going to get to do something fun, hurt a man who had been stupidly hurting others, and get to work with the family. Evan had been standing back and allowing her to do what she needed to get it done. Then at the last minute, he'd been called away for a medical emergency.

She had expected Evan to balk at the idea of her going in alone with a known rapist. She was armed, and knew skills that would protect all of them should the need arise. But he'd deferred to her ability and knowledge of this sort of thing, and she couldn't have loved him more for it.

Her name was called to be closed up in the office of Ed Baldwin for a job interview.

"Hello, my dear. You sure are a pretty little thing, aren't you? I don't believe I've seen you here before, have I?" She said she was new to town. "Well, that explains it. Come, have a seat and we'll talk. I'm to understand that you're here for the substitute teacher position."

"Yes, I was looking for a job." He picked up her application and looked it over while she continued. "But I have no desire to be your plaything, nor be drugged up and raped when I'm out of it."

He stared at her for several seconds before he put the paper down and stood up. She told him to sit and not to move. It was empowering for her to see him do just what she told him.

"I don't know what the meaning of this is, but I would like for you to leave my office right now." She pulled out her gun and set it on the desk between them. "You're in violation of several laws right now, and I'm going to call the police."

"That's good, but they're here already." He looked nervous now. "You're going to tell me what you were doing and why. Then they're going to come in here and arrest you. It's simple, really. Tit for tat. However, you'll notice that there are no tits for you to grab or fondle."

"Where are you getting these lies? You know what, I don't care. You're going to jail for slander." She told him it would have to be false if that were the case. "It is. I don't...I would like for you to leave my office this minute. And to think.... You came in here under false pretenses. I want you out of here."

"You're not going to confess? That really sucks. I had a bet with my husband — well, my husband to be — that you'd cough it right up. Now it looks like I'm going to have to get rough with you." He stood up. "Don't you have, I don't know, something in your desk that I could find and this will be done? They told me that I can't hurt you unless you're hurting me. I hate rules like that, but do you have pictures or something?"

He looked to his left and she did as well. Then he started telling her to leave again. But she knew as surely as he was standing there that there was something of a memento of his hurting those women. Getting up, she went to the wall and saw it right away. The little camera eye was cleverly hidden, but easy to spot if you knew what to look for.

Dylan wanted to confront him again, get him to say whatever was needed to get him out of here, but this would be so much stronger of a case. To have him caught with the goods, so to speak. As she was going to the door, he started for the wall and she stopped him by picking up her gun.

"Move and the trial will be short and sweet. It won't be as much fun if you're dead, but it will be much shorter." He put his hands up and started sobbing about how unfair she was being. Opening the door, she let the police in, as well as Adrian. She wished that Evan was here as well, but he told her that she could do this and she believed that she could. And would.

The police were taking their time about everything. She wanted them to rip out the wall, find whatever it was that he was hiding and be done with it. That's what she might have done. As they wandered around the room, just talking about nothing, she had enough. When Adrian stepped in front of her as she was headed to the wall she'd found out about, she wanted to smack him as well.

"They're not doing shit." He asked her what they could do. "I don't know, arrest him? Go and find out what he has in that wall?"

"They're waiting on a search warrant." She didn't like it but understood. "Once they have that, we can rip out walls, tear this man a new ass, and end this. But—and I'm sure you know this—without due process, we won't have a leg to stand on when he comes up for trial."

"He didn't confess." Adrian said it was going to matter little. "But don't you have to have something to make the judge give you a warrant to go through this place?"

"Ah, but we do. Three of the women that I spoke to yesterday have written out what they remember happening in here. And with that, he'll write us one. You did great work."

She asked him how. "Well, first of all, you didn't kill him. When you pulled out your gun, I was sure he was a goner. And you found the camera. Without that, we might have only had their word."

It wasn't perfect, but she supposed it was good. As they stood around she looked at the office. It was nice. There were lots of windows around the room, as well as bookshelves with a great many books, pictures in small frames, and other things on them. While she was standing in front of one particular shelf, two things on the shelf seemed to jump out at her.

"Adrian?" He stood next to her and she watched his face as he took in the shelf she was pointing too. The longer she stood there, the more she wanted to turn to Ed and blow his fucking brains out. When Adrian looked at her again, she knew that he saw them.

"Mother fuck." He turned then, just as she pulled her gun. As Adrian went from man to beast, she fired a shot. Ed went down...not because she'd hit him, but because of Adrian. Hell was going to be paid before this ended, she knew it.

Adrian held Ed down with his mouth around this throat. The other men, all police, stood still, and she realized that they'd known that he was a tiger. Walking to the cat and man, she knelt to their level and looked at the face of Ed. He wasn't moving, even to blink.

"You're a sick fucker, anyone ever tell you that?" He didn't move and she looked at the shelf. "You thought if you put it out in plain sight that no one would notice? Or did you get your jollies by knowing that they were right there for anyone to see?"

"Ma'am? Can you please tell us what's going on?" She

stood then, knowing that Adrian wouldn't kill Ed but he'd not move either. "We understand that it's bad, otherwise Adrian wouldn't have shifted. Can you help us?"

Dylan walked to the shelf that they'd taken pictures of as soon as they entered the room and pulled the two pictures down and handed them to the officer. It took him more time than it had either her or Adrian, but he saw it. Handing the pictures of the little boys to his fellow officers, he held his gun on Ed and asked Adrian to let him go.

"Jesus H. Christ. He killed them." The man holding the pictures looked sick. Not that she blamed him. "I've been in here numerous times and never.... Christ almighty."

The pictures were of two little boys about ten or younger. Ed was in the photos with them. Each of them looked like a picture of a man with a boy smiling into the camera. Until you looked at it hard. The knives in the children's chests were there to see, and the blood down the front of their shirts was dark in the black and white photos. And Ed wasn't kissing them on the cheek but licking them, and the blood that was there as well. The pictures were very telling of the sort of man Ed really was.

Ten minutes after the warrant to search was brought, men were brought in to tear out the wall. The entire thing was recorded by the police, and other agencies were called in to bear witness. By the time they had gotten to not just the video camera and recordings, but thousands of pictures as well, Ed had been arrested and taken away. Adrian had made his way to a room to shift and redress.

Not only were there more pictures of women, but they found a stash of pictures of small boys, all of them very young, and two more pictures of the children that had been put out on display. They showed not only the man killing them, but how he'd masturbated on their dead bodies as well.

"I'd like to talk to you." Adrian told the mayor, Marlin Hoover, that he was busy right now. "No. Right now, if you please. I need to get this right so when I go on television, I can have all the facts straight."

"*You* want to get the facts right? Why do you want to get the credit for what he's done?" Hoover asked Dylan to please lower her voice. "I don't think so. This was all on him. Had you been in charge, you wouldn't have found shit. Adrian found the trouble and did something about it. While you, you fat tub of lard, sat back on your ass and didn't do shit."

"Are you going to let her talk to me this way, Adrian? You and I have a good working relationship. I'd hate for her to mess that up for you." Adrian didn't answer, but he did smile. "Your future might be in jeopardy if you let her sound off like this."

"In the event that you didn't notice, she's a grown woman and can speak her own mind. And if you threaten either one of us again, I'll have your ass hauled before the committee so quickly that you won't remember the trip over." Dylan watched the mayor walk away grumbling. "I think I might like taking his job."

"His job? Well, good for you. You'd be perfect." Adrian moved away too, answering questions that were posed to him by the police and news crews.

Are you all right? She told Evan that she was. *I just spoke to Dad. He said there was a shakeup at the principal's office. I'm guessing things went the way they were planned.*

More than that. They're going to get the guy on child pornography, as well as murder. Evan asked her what had happened and she told him. *There are going to be a lot of unsolved murders of children closed today, I think. Christ, when I think of all those families he hurt.*

She told Evan what she'd seen and how it came to light. The police, she explained, were taking this one by the books, and it was frustrating for her. Evan told her that justice would be served in the right way, and not by jumping in too soon and no one getting any kind of closure.

I don't have to like it. He said that he didn't either, but at least some of it was solved. *I suppose so. Adrian is talking to the police now.*

He's very upset. She thought that was an understatement and told him. *Is it because of this or something else?*

The mayor wanted him to give up all the details so that he could take credit for the findings. Adrian...I have to tell you, Evan, I never thought he had it in him. Adrian spoke to him all soft-like and smiling, but there was an underlying threat and current that made me want to take a step back. It was like he was showing a side of himself that he never lets anyone see. I think he'd make a great mayor. Evan said that he'd always known that Adrian had grit, as his grandpa had called it, but had never seen it. *He's running for mayor, I think. And I bet I know who we have to thank for that.*

Henry. They both laughed. *I should be done here in a couple of hours. My patient is doing well, but I don't want to leave until he's awake and talking.*

I'm so proud of you. He told her that he was equally proud of her. *We make a hell of a team, I think. And you'll be happy to know that I didn't shoot anyone today. Adrian said he thought that I would when I had to draw my gun.*

I am happy about that. Good for you. Evan laughed again, and it rang in her mind well after he told her he had to go.

133

When Ollie and Oliver showed up half an hour later, the police were waiting on the Feds. Apparently, they were making sure that not only were they doing things by the books, but were also calling in backup to make sure that they were cataloging the right way and that there were no mistakes on this one. Since it was on state property, they weren't taking any chances. No one was, it seemed.

By midnight the school was closed, the grounds were being guarded, and the police and Feds were trying to make heads or tails out of the pictures and tapes they'd found. Dylan thought it was going to be a long time before any of this was figured out.

CHAPTER 10

The house was coming along nicely. As Evan walked through it, he saw walls up where there hadn't been any before. Wiring was complete, as well as extra outlets put where he'd suggested. And the flooring in the living room, as well as the dining room, was being sanded down to the original wood. He loved the way it was coming together.

"I've been looking for you." He smiled at his dad. "My goodness, boy. I think you might be spending more on this house than it would have cost you to get a new one."

"Dylan loves this house, and so do I. We would never have been able to get this much charm in a new one anyway." His dad agreed. "What did you need? Or did you only want to bust my chops?"

"Both. But I really did need you in the hallway on the second floor. I was looking around and I found something you might be a bit interested in." As they took the stairs, Dad was telling him. "I was standing outside, just looking up, when I noticed that the house was off. Not bad off, just not proportioned like I thought it should be. So, I had me a little look-see. It took me some doing, but I found an old door that had been shut off. I'd say a long time ago too."

The doorway had been busted open in the hallway, and Evan could see that it had been made to look like just another part of the wall. His dad told him that it looked as if someone had boarded it up to close off this part of the house. As soon as they entered the area, he knew just what it was.

"It's the staff quarters." Dad said that he thought Evan might be right. "Look how small these rooms are. There had to be some kind of back stairs here as well, so they'd never be seen by the residents, don't you think?"

There were six bedrooms along the long hall, all of them no bigger than the space it would take to put a full-sized bed. Each of the rooms had a single cot like bed, pegs on the walls, and a chair. The light was a single bulb that hung from the ceiling that turned off and on by a pull string.

"There's a single bathroom down at the end, as well as a place that I can only assume was a sort of kitchen. There are a lot of tea sets in there too. If you decide to get rid of them, I'd like them for your momma. She sure would love them." He told Dad that he'd talk to Dylan, but he didn't see any reason why he couldn't have them. "I'll buy them. They're pretty little things."

They explored the entire area. Evan thought there were some nice pieces that he'd like to see incorporated in the other rooms of the house. The claw footed tub was beautiful. There was a brick fireplace that he wanted to somehow preserve, as well as the cups that his dad wanted, two dozen in all. The tea pots that they found in the cupboard in the room were matched up with them. When Dylan showed up, she told Dad to take them all.

"You should get something for them. I mean, they might be as old as this house." Dylan told him she was getting something, the pleasure of letting someone else enjoy them. "Well, she'll surely love you for it. Not that she doesn't already. Lordy, you'll have to have a tea with her sometime. Or coffee. That would make her day."

The tub was beautiful and could be used in the master bathroom. The large chamber pots, as well as some pieces of kitchenware they found, were also boxed up and moved out of the room. Then they found the linen closet.

There weren't just sheets and towels in it, but also things like combs and brushes. A curling iron that had to be heated up on the stove. Combs for the hair that were works of art. And there were napkins and tablecloths that had been handstitched and wrapped in burlap.

"We should donate some of these things. I don't know who would want them, but there has to be someplace that has some history on this house and the town." Dad told Dylan that there used to be a place downtown, but it shut up a few years ago when the curator had passed. "Your wife belongs to one of those women's groups, doesn't she? Maybe she can find someone to open it and run it. It's a shame that all this stuff might be put away for no one to see."

"She might be able to twist some arms to get it going again." Evan wasn't sure what Mom would say to Dad's claim about her methods, but he wisely said nothing. Within an hour, not only were the tea sets packed up, but the rest of the wing was as well. Evan thought they could change the rooms into something like storage space.

"The thought of these poor women cooped up in these

tiny rooms just breaks my heart." Evan told his mom that they would have thought themselves very lucky to have had a job. "I guess so. And I'm sure that they spent a great deal of their time downstairs working. What do you suppose it would take to find someone that might have worked here at one time? I would love to talk to them. The stories might go nicely with some of these things you've found."

"I'll have David look into it. He does that sort of research all the time for his books. Maybe he'll write one about them." David would be more interested in the romance story that would have gone along with this place. Weaving a story that would have had love blooming in the upstairs maids' room. "He might even find something on the entire house."

The house was being worked on all the time now. Evan thought that instead of a couple of months like he'd been told, they might be moving in a few weeks from now. He hoped so. It would be nice to have his own bed and his own things around him. Right now, living with his parents was nice, but there was no alone time for him and Dylan.

Dylan was in the master bedroom with one of the workers when he found her. She was describing what she wanted in the way of the closet. Shelves all down one side, and room for a gun cabinet. It was going to be tricky, the man told her, but he'd do it. When he left to find out the specs on the cabinet she wanted, Dylan looked at him.

"Did you know that once you put in a gun cabinet the size that I want, all kinds of rules have to be set up?" He said that he didn't. "Well, there are. One of them is that you have to learn to shoot them. And the family."

"I don't think I've ever heard that rule. But I like it. Come here, I need to touch you." She willingly came to his embrace. As he held her, he thought of all the things he wanted to do to her. "We should stay here tonight. Just to make sure that the floors and walls are as soundproof as we want them to be."

"Excellent idea. I know that the bedroom could use a little of your expertise. Also, did you see the bathroom? How on earth were we thinking that we needed such a huge space?" Evan followed her into the room and was surprised by the sheer size of it. "We could all take a shower in this stall and never touch. Not that I don't want you touching me, but sheesh, this is huge."

"I thought it would be nice to make love in here." He pressed her to the wall to show her. "See, plenty of room for me to take you hard here. Or even to be on my knees eating you. I'm betting even my cat wouldn't mind the water so long as he was tasting his mate."

Evan could smell her then. She was aroused. And when he licked her neck, he could taste it on her, the dewy need that was like a fine wine. He rocked into her and was rewarded with a deep moan from her.

"I need you." Nodding, he started pulling her clothing off. "Now, hurry, before I just combust with a climax."

She was naked before he was, which suited him just fine... he could taste her while he pulled off the rest of his clothing. But before he could do more than free his cock, she was down on her knees in front of him. And when she wrapped her hand around him, it was all he could do not to come all over her.

Her mouth moved like her body did when she was sitting over him. Smoothly, touching him in places that would feel branded by her touch. And when she took him into her mouth, he held onto the walls of the stall, praying that he didn't embarrass himself by coming too soon. But the way she was taking him, Evan knew that he wasn't going to last long.

~~~

Dylan had never enjoyed giving oral sex before. They were usually so ready to fuck her throat that she simply hurried them along so that she could breathe. But with Evan, it was wonderful. Fulfilling and sexy.

Every time he moaned, moved his cock further into her mouth, she wanted more. His hand in her hair made her want to take him deeper, let him come all over her as well as in her mouth. When he pulled her away, telling her that he was too close, she wrapped her hand around his balls and rolled them. It was all it took to have him coming all over her face and breasts.

Before she could relish the feeling of having his hot cum all over her, she was up on her feet and bent over the counter. His cock filled her painfully, hard strokes that made her dizzy with need. And when he jerked her head back, her body spooned against his, she came hard enough to see stars, her body tight with her release.

He tore at her shoulder then. His canines were sharp, more so than she'd ever felt them before. And when she watched him in the mirror, she saw his cat, his fur racing over his skin like her climax had. Screaming out another release—they were coming so quick, they were back to back—she held onto him. And when he ordered her to come again, she did so but blacked out when she screamed.

When she woke, Dylan was on the floor wrapped in one of the sheets that they'd brought over to use as paint drops. Evan was standing at the window, his phone pressed to his ear as he appeared to be listening. His tone was low, his body stiff.

Whatever had happened, he wasn't happy about it. As soon as he closed the connection, he turned and looked at her.

"My patient died." She told him she was so sorry. "I am as well. He was doing well when I left, but he had a stroke that killed him. There wasn't anything we could have done for him even had I been there with him."

"I'm so very sorry. I know how you love each of your patients." She got up and pulled her clothing on. When she was dressed, she walked to him and wrapped her arms around his waist. "What was the surgery? I mean, that wasn't it, was it?"

"I don't think so. Not directly, anyway. He was warned before I did it that there might be complications. He was well over what could have been considered a good weight. His blood pressure had been high for a long time. The surgery I performed was to set his leg that had been broken a few months ago, and he'd never had it looked at. The break was giving him too much pain for him to even step on his foot." Evan held her in his arms when he turned. "That was my nurse that called me. She said that his family wasn't surprised by his death, but they were taking it very hard."

"Understandable. It's difficult to lose anyone that you love." Evan nodded and held her tighter. "What is it you have to do now? Go back into the city?"

"Yes. I was just going to wake you to let you know. Would you like to go with me?" She looked up at him and smiled. "I don't think that's the answer I was hoping for."

"I have to be with your brother when he talks to the media in the morning. I made a promise. He said that he'll talk to them, but he wants moral support. And I was there with him so they might, which I doubt, have questions for me as well." He said he understood. "I can meet you there later. We still have to pick out furniture for the living room, right?"

"Yes. I have things in my apartment, but I don't think any of it will be suitable for the new house. Not to mention, it's only a chair and an end table. I didn't spend a lot of time there other than to sleep." They worked out a time to meet and where, and then he kissed her. "I need to see about getting you a car. I know that you can come in with one of my brothers or in the limo, but it would be better if you could drive."

"I'm fine." And she was too. "Besides, I think a car would just get me into trouble. I've been known for my tendencies of driving too fast."

He kissed her and told her to behave, and then he left. It wasn't that far of a drive, but he didn't want to go. As soon as he was gone, Dylan walked around the empty house. Christ, it was fucking huge.

The kitchen was well on its way to being complete. The dining room was nearly so, but they had to wait on the door that she and Evan had decided to put in. She had thought a window would have been lovely, but Evan said it would be nice to have a way to spill the room out onto the deck beyond. Once the door was in, the drywall on that wall would go up and then it would be painted.

She loved the style of the living room. There was a double fireplace that could also be used in the library. Standing in front of the stone facade, she thought of all the pictures that she wanted to display here. And the holidays spent in this room with family.

Just as she was headed to the study, her mom and dad showed up. Dylan spent the next hour showing them the improvements they were doing to the old home.

"This is going to be such a grand home." Her mom asked about furniture. "I know that you'll want new, but there are some things in storage that were your grandparents'. If you don't want it, we could probably put it somewhere else."

"No. I completely forgot about it. There were two couches that were Grandmas, right?" Mom told her that one of them was a fainting couch. "That's wonderful. And her dining room table and chairs. I think it would fit in with ours here."

"It's massive, honey. I believe there are a dozen side chairs, as well as one on each end." Dylan took them to that room again after finding a tape measure. "I think it'll fit nicely in here. And you'll have the two china cabinets that match it as well. Dylan, your grandparents would be so proud of you right now."

"Grandda was here yesterday. He said that he'd help with the yard. I think one of the men working out there set him to work on the roses. Grandpa was having a great time, it looked like."

Dad told her that he'd slept like a log after coming home. "And he said that you bought him lunch. I'm sorry that he thinks that you're just some stranger at times." Dylan looked at her dad and smiled, wondering how much it hurt him to have his dad not know him either. "He forgets me too most of the time."

"It's all right, Dad. He more than makes up for it when he's having a good day. Just a few days ago, he told me about one of his first jobs as a carpet delivery person. He said the things people would do with their old carpets was amazing. I guess some of them used them in the gardens to keep the weeds down." His dad laughed and said that they'd tried a few of

143

them when he was a kid. "I miss him, but I'm thankful that we have him."

"Yes, so am I. And with the added help, it makes it easier too." Dylan was glad that Evan had helped her parents out with the nurses. They were not as stressed all the time from having no time for each other. "We were going to go with you to the press conference. I'm glad that you and Adrian were able to get this taken care of. But those poor people. I can't imagine what they've been through all this time."

She went to the Whitfield home to shower and change. While there, she talked to Ollie about the house and grabbed a quick breakfast. They were on their way to the courthouse when she thought of the mayor. She hoped that Adrian had done what he said he was going to do to make everyone see that the mayor was a fraud.

The podium was set up, and there were hundreds of people waiting to hear the update on the school. There was an absence of children, she noticed right away. School was still out, but she figured that no one would want their kids to hear why. As she made her way to Adrian, she saw Marlin there talking to him. She didn't say anything as she stood near her future brother-in-law.

"You have anything written down for me?" Adrian told him that he'd not thought of that. "Well, it'll certainly help me when they ask me questions. I'm glad that we worked things out with this. It wouldn't go well if you were to stand up there and freeze up. The governor is here too, and he's got it in his head that you should speak first. Remember what I told you, Adrian, just tell them that you helped me gather things up, but I'm the one that made it happen."

144

"You don't have to worry about me, Marlin. I got it." She started to protest, but Adrian winked at her as he continued with Marlin. "I have been working on this all night. I didn't want to mess up and have you threaten me and my family again."

"Well, sometimes people don't know what this job entails. You have to be strong and willing to say things that you'd not normally say. You just keep to the program, Adrian, and we'll get along just fine." When Marlin walked away, shaking hands with anyone stupid enough not to turn their backs on him, she looked at Adrian.

"Don't give me that look. I do know what I'm doing. The governor called me last night, and then again this morning after I sent him a report of what I did and why." She asked him how that had gone over. "He's very upset...it's why he's here. I even told him how Marlin threatened me, in addition to all the things I've done for him over the last few months. I guess the reports that he got are very different than my side of the story."

The room quieted as soon as he was given the signal to go up and talk. Adrian looked around, then glanced at her before he addressed the crowd. Dylan saw that there were about eight newscasters here, as well as some newspapers that were being represented. He was either going to throw up, it looked to her, or run like his life depended on it. When he cleared his throat and smiled, Dylan knew he was going to be just fine.

"Good morning, everyone. My name is Adrian Whitfield. I'm going to tell you what I can about the situation that I came across yesterday. My grandpa had mentioned some time ago about the teachers leaving our fine schools. Several of them even picked up and left the area without any form of explanation. It

145

was—"

"Wait, wait, wait." Everyone turned to Marlin. His nervous laughter made her want to puke on him. "I think you've been letting this go all to your head, young man. I know you helped, but you're making it sound as if you were the only one that worked on this. And I'm the one that noticed the teachers leaving. Tell them that."

"No, I don't think so. And if you threaten me again, I'll press charges." Dylan had to stifle a laugh. The current mayor looked like he'd been caught with his hand in the cookie jar. "As I was saying, the teachers were leaving faster than we could find replacements. It wasn't until I had my sister-in-law help me out with a sting sort of operation that—"

"I think you need to step back, Adrian." Adrian stood there, saying nothing as Marlin tried to physically push him out of the way. It wasn't until someone from the back of the room spoke up that he looked angry.

"You need to let him tell us what happened." The mayor said he'd tell them. "All right. You go right ahead. We'd like for you to explain when you first noticed the staff leaving and what you did about it."

"Well, I went to Adrian here and had him do some investigations. It's what we pay him for." The man asked when he'd done this. "When? I'd have to check my calendar on that."

His secretary handed him a thick binder. From the look on his face, Dylan would bet anything that the woman would be fired before the end of the day. As Marlin made a big show of going through his calendar, Shelly, the secretary, told him he wasn't going to find it.

"I don't remember." The man said that something this big,

146

he'd remember. "Well, as I was telling Adrian here, I have a lot of things on my plate."

"So, the murder of children and the raping of their teachers, that holds no special place in your mind? It certainly would mine." Dylan saw the man talking then, and laughed. Marlin turned and glared at her when she did, and she lifted her chin. Ollie Whitfield was having the time of his life embarrassing the mayor. "You said you paid young Adrian there. How does that work? I mean, if you're paying him, I think someone would have mentioned that. Adrian? Is he paying you?"

Shaking his head, he pushed his way to the microphone again. "He's supposed to, but he's in arrears for about six months now." When no one stopped him, he continued. "I helped with the playground addition at the school. The mayor approached me about using some of the funds that were left over at the end of the year. It wasn't much, a few hundred dollars. I have no idea what happened to the rest of it. Nor did I have any idea when I started the project that thousands of dollars of that money that had been leftover had been earmarked for a new teachers' lounge that had been approved, as well as new tables for the lunchroom. So, in an effort to get things done and to do something for the kids, I paid for the additional cost on my own. The lounge and tables are still not taken care of as of this morning when I went by to have a look. As I'm sure any of the teachers can attest to the fact that there is a great need for those tables, and for the teachers to have a safe place to go and unwind during the day."

The governor came out of the crowd and made his way to the podium. When Marlin moved to intercept him, he was literally pushed out of the way. Governor Wilson thanked

Adrian and told him he was proud of him. Then they answered questions as Marlin was hauled away by the police.

CHAPTER 11

Evan hated shopping for the most part. If he could order something online, he'd do that rather than man the malls. Or any department store for that matter. But shopping with Dylan had a special kind of fun attached to it. They were buying things for their new home together. He entered the kitchen area just as she was pulling down plates and laying them on the table set up there.

"You have a very large family." He told her she did as well. "Yes, well, I don't know how we're ever going to fit in our dining room when they all come to visit. My family will take up three places, while yours takes...let me see, eight. With you and I, that's just enough to fit at the table. Until they have mates and children."

"The wall still isn't up. We could have them expand the room to accommodate a custom-made table that will hold fifty." She glared. "I don't know if you're aware of this or not, but I think you're incredibly sexy when you have that look about you."

"You think me being upset with you is sexy?" He nodded and grinned at the next look she gave him. "I think you're off your rocker, and I think if we ask those men to move one more wall, they'll quit. We'll figure out something."

He already had, and it was being worked on now. The room was not just made wider, but longer as well, not just to accommodate the table from her grandparents, but a hutch from his grandparents, and built-in china cabinets that went with the table she had inherited. His mom and Stella had been surprised that each of the sets, from different homes, had matched perfectly. The room would be more than large enough to hold family gatherings.

"Evan?" He felt his cat move over him at the tone of her voice. It was low, sort of pitched with a little fear. "Where is everyone?"

He looked around. It was the first time he'd noticed that not only were they alone on this floor, but even the cashiers were missing. Evan moved deeper into the room and leaned into her ear to ask her if she was armed. When she nodded, he didn't know if he was relieved or more afraid. Something was going on.

"How many people were up here when we got here?" She told him that she'd seen a dozen at least. "And when we went into the restrooms, did you see anyone when you came out? I didn't, but it never struck me as odd."

"No, now that I think about it. Two women came in the bathroom while I was in there. I could hear them talking about some sales person that was walking the store. Then when I left, I didn't see them but figured that they were on another floor." He nodded and looked around to see if he could see anything. Just as he was going to tell her that they were leaving, his dad spoke to him.

Where are you? He told him. *I know that…what floor? Are you in this mess? Christ almighty, son, it's a muddle.*

Dylan and I are on the fourth floor. We came up here about an hour ago. What's going on, Dad? Evan told Dylan he was speaking to his dad and nearly missed what he said. *I'm sorry, what?*

The place is in lockdown. There is a man, or maybe a couple of them, that has a gun on the workers and other people. I heard there were about two dozen shoppers and employees, but I don't think that's right. Too big for only that few, don't you think? He didn't know, but asked his dad where they were. *Best anyone can tell, the main lobby. I'll try and figure out what I can. Your momma and I came in to surprise you two and have some dinner. You be safe, both of you, and I'll be back.*

He told Dylan what his dad had said. "He said he'd get back with me when he could. He's trying to find out what's going on. He wants us to stay up here."

"And do what? Wait for those people to be killed? I can't do that." He wanted to tell Dylan she had to, for him, but she was right. Those people might even be hurt, and he could help them. "I'm going to go down easy and you stay here."

"I'm going as well. I might not be able to help them like you will be able to, but if anyone is hurt and needs a doctor, I can help them." He was going to follow her regardless, but Evan was glad when she nodded. "I don't have my bag, but I can work if need be. Plus, I have my beast."

"You should see if anyone down there is someone you know. It would help to get a better perspective on what we're going to go into."

He nodded and reached out. It was difficult. He wasn't sure who to be looking for, then he remembered Mrs. Galley.

She worked the elevators on the lower floors. And as part of the leap, she had already formed a link with him.

Oh Evan, honey, I can't talk now. I'm in a pickle of a deal here. He told her that he was in the building. *You are? Well, you stay out of sight. There are some men here that are just about to murder us all. Oh Lordy.*

I have my wife with me, and she's armed. Special Forces, and we're going to help. She told him they'd be hurt. *No. Not if you think you can help us. How many men are there? Where are you?*

We're on the first floor in the back. They got...let me think a minute. You have to be careful. Your poor momma will skin you alive if you get yourself hurt. He told her that he was being extra careful. *There are three men in here with us, and two or more at the front of the place. They're armed, they are. And I don't know, but I think they might be related. Something about a job.*

He told Dylan. "Ask her if they have masks on. There's no money, not much I'd think. Not with credit cards being used as much as they are nowadays. Who are they waiting on? There has to be a reason that they've not killed anyone yet, or left."

Mrs. Galley? What did you hear for their reason for coming in? I mean, there can't be that much in the way of cash in the place. And Dylan wants to know if they're masked. If they've said who they're waiting on. She said she would see what she could figure out. *Be careful. My mom will skin you alive if you're hurt too.*

Your momma, she's a pistol. She was quiet for a long time. Evan knew that she was still there, he could feel her fear and her excitement about helping them. When she came back to him, he repeated everything she told him to Dylan.

Mick Daniels was fired three days ago. These men are his family. They want someone to pay for his being fired. Evan asked if Mick was with them. *No. Apparently, he committed suicide yesterday. They're here for his boss. I don't believe he's here either. That's what has them so riled up. They're gonna start shooting soon, to make him come here and turn himself over to them. And Evan, they're wolves.*

That made a world of difference. "If we hurt them, they'll shift and come back at us. If we kill them, they'll be naked when they come back and there will be questions. I don't know if I can kill them, Dylan. I'm a doctor. I'm not saying that we can't do anything, but I don't know how much help I can be."

"You've already been more help than you know. We have knowledge of not just where they are, but how many there are of them. We know names, reasons, and that they're armed. Not just with guns, but with their beasts as well. Without you and your friend, we'd be walking into a nightmare that we might not have survived." He nodded, but was still unsure. "I'm going to try my best to talk them out of this shit. But I won't have those people dying because they're stupid. All right?"

"Yes, but I want you to be careful. And if that means they die, then that's fine so long as you're with me at the end of the day." She pulled him to her and kissed him. It was what he needed. "When do we go?"

"Now."

They used the stairs instead of the elevator. The noise, he knew, would alert them that there were others in the place. As they entered the lowest level, he told his dad what they were doing and what Mrs. Galley had told him. Dad told him to be careful as well. He also said he'd contact the local alpha and let him know.

The door opened without a sound. Dylan disappeared out the door before he could tell her once again to be careful. Evan stood in the corridor of the shaft they were in and let out a long breath.

The plan was solid. She would go in first, see the lay of the land, then he'd try his best to lead as many people away as he could. If he needed to shift, she had suggested that he strip first, in the event that he needed to get back into his clothing when they left. He saw Dylan at the end of the hall that led into the shopping area. It was now or never, he supposed.

~~~

Dylan could smell the men and wondered about that, but right now she had to work. Their wolves were making it easier for her to track where they were. The scent, their scent, got stronger the closer she got to them. As she rounded the display of menswear, she saw the group of people on the floor with their hands on their laps. Mrs. Galley looked right at her and nodded once. Dylan reached for Evan to get help.

I see her. Ask her to tell me, like she's at six o'clock on the face of a watch, where they are. Also, there are about twenty hostages, including four children. Dylan received the information and walked into the melee with her gun above her head.

"Hello, boys." They all turned to her at once. Their guns were pointed at her now instead of the hostages. That was the plan with Evan. He was going to sneak out who he could. "I want you to know that I'm not alone. And if you try and shoot me, you'll be dead before I hit the floor."

"What the fuck are you doing in here? How did you...? Where the fuck is everyone else?" She just smiled at the first man. "Who are you?"

"Now, does that really matter? No, it doesn't. What does matter is that you're going down for a lot of things right now.

Kidnapping. Armed robbery." He told her that they didn't take anything. "No, perhaps you haven't taken anything physically. But you did ruin a lot of things. That sofa has a bullet hole in it. There are a few damaged displays. That makes it robbery since you did it without paying first. Also, and here is where it's going to hurt you the most, they'll charge you for time lost. You know, all these employees are supposed to be working. Those customers can't buy anything if you're detaining them. It all adds up. I'm thinking perhaps as much as ten million dollars. At least."

"You sure about that?" She nodded. Dylan wasn't sure about any of it, but it made them pay attention to her instead of the hostages. "How about you make a call or something and get the manager down here? He killed my brother by firing him."

"What reason did your brother give you for being fired?" The man looked at the others before looking at her again. "You know that it's going to come out. You might as well tell me."

She saw Evan waving for some of the people to come to him. She didn't know how many he'd gotten out already, but she thought there were less in the group. When two got up and went to him carefully, she looked at the men.

"He told him that he'd been late too many times. Mick, he don't have a car, so he had to walk to work." She asked if any of them had a car. "I do, but I got me no reason to take him to work. That was his way of things."

"Oh, so you got him fired." The man pointed the gun at her again. "You had a car but wouldn't help your own brother out by taking him to work. Did he ask you? Offer to pay for your gas?"

"Yeah, but it's my car, not his. I worked on it and made it

running." She sat down on one of the beds. Making sure that her gun was ready, she shook her head. "You think it's my fault? I don't. I told you, it was my car."

"So you said. Now, because he's gone, you think to come in here and do what...kill his boss for trying to make his business work? Your momma must be ashamed of you about right now." Two of the men dropped their heads in shame. "Look at her little boys now. All of you are going to jail on top of her losing her son. What do you think is going to happen to her now that you're fucking up so badly that she'll be all alone?"

"We're going to go back home when we're done here." She shook her head. "Yeah, we are. We're gonna help her out by making this right."

"Making what right? By killing off this man, you think that's gonna bring your brother back? It won't, in case you didn't know. And she's gonna only see you for the second or two that the police let her. I'm pretty sure by now they know not only who you are but why you're here, as well as where you each live. I don't see you getting to go back home at all." He told her she was lying. "Am I? Well, here's what I know. You're James. Your brothers are Willie, Ben, Davey, and Carter. Not only are you going to jail, but you've fucked up with your alpha too. You think he's going to be thrilled that you've come in here without his permission?"

She'd gotten the names from Evan, who had gotten them from his dad. This three-way talking was slightly confusing, but it was working. And the alpha was outside too, and he was spitting mad.

"How do you know us? We were careful not to let anyone know who we was." She told him it was a small town and everyone knew everyone. "We'll just kill them all off. Even you. That way no one can tell on us."

"Your alpha is out there and he knows. Ask him." James was quiet for a few minutes, and when two of the brothers put down their weapons, she wondered if the rest of them would. "You're in deep shit, buddy."

The two that had put down their weapons dropped to the floor, their hands over their heads and linked at the fingers. She watched the other two men, and when they did the same, it left James all by himself. But she had a feeling that he wasn't going to cooperate.

"Put down the gun and no one will have to die." He said that he was going to kill them all. "You try that and you'll never get the opportunity to lift your gun to them. Put down your weapon and everyone lives for another day."

"I can't do that." She told him that he could. But when he lifted his gun up and pointed at her, she did the same and watched him. "They need to pay for him dying. I want someone to tell me that they're sorry my brother is dead."

"I am sorry. But again, that's not going to bring him back. And neither will you dying. Just lower your weapon, James, and you'll only go to jail, not six feet under."

The gun went off. The pain seared through her arm, but she fired her weapon before she let the pain take her. James dropped to the floor even as the last of the hostages was taken out by Evan. Dylan sat where she was until he came toward her.

"I thought you said you'd not get hurt." She kissed him and told him she was fine. "Sure you are. And the blood that is all over you, I suppose that's fine too."

"It's not a head or heart shot, so I should live." She held his hand. "We should tell everyone the coast is clear."

"In a second. I need to be with you." She nodded and looked at the four men still sitting on the floor. "They're going to die, you know that, don't you?"

"I figured as much. What about their mom? She'll not be caught up in their mess, will she?" He told her he had no idea. "We need a cook, don't we? I mean, we could hire her to do something for us. Petition for her release or whatever it's called."

"I'll talk to Nathan; Nathan Briggs is their alpha." She nodded and heard the doors explode open. "They'll arrest you, Dad said."

"Yes, they will, but I have to make sure that they don't shoot me too. Go over there and don't move. And listen to everything they tell you." She got down on her knees and put her weapons in front of her. All of them, including the knife she had in her boot. Then she put her hands up over her head with her Army ID out where they could see it.

It went just as she thought it would. The police were taking no chances, and had one of their men holding a gun on her. She didn't mind so long as they didn't get trigger happy. Once they had everything and everyone in lock down, Evan told them where the people were. She stayed right where she was.

The body was taken away. The hostages were put into a large room and held there until they could be talked to. Evan made sure that none of them were injured while she answered questions. He'd already patched her arm up—it had really only been a through and through—but he was concerned enough to tell the police if they upset her, he'd kill them. Then he simply walked away.

For a man that told her that he'd not be able to kill anyone, his threat was very convincing. Each person that sat down next to her to start questions asked her if she was all right or if she needed something.

The alpha, Nathan, came in after a few minutes. He did look like a wolf, from his shaggy hair to his big frame. She'd not fuck with him. As he stood over the four remaining men, she watched him to see if he was going to harm them now.

"You acted with violence to humans. You know the penalty for that." Each man nodded. "If not for the help of the leap woman and her mate, you'd be dead now. Now, because of your actions, you are no longer in this pack. Your mother will be shunned as well because of what happened here."

"Excuse me." Nathan turned to her and she saw his anger, like a coat of armor. She stood up and told him who she was. "My name is Dylan Whitfield. Sergeant First Class of the United States Armed Forces."

"You're mated to Evan Whitfield." She nodded at his statement. "I am aware that you are new to his leap, but these men are to answer for crimes against our kind. And in doing so, they will be dealt with as I see fit."

"Good. I mean, they're dumb asses if they thought this had any other outcome than what you're going to do to them. Honestly, I thought for sure you'd have them killed." He said that remained to be seen. "I was going to ask you...well, Evan and I were going to ask you if we might.... You're right, sir, I'm new to all of this, but I would ask you for something. I'd like to hire these idiots' mom to work for us. If you toss her out, which is your right to do so, I'd like to make sure that she's taken care of. I have a grandfather, he's having.... My grandda is lost sometimes with Alzheimer's, and I would hope that someone would care for him like these fools should have their mother."

"I've seen your grandfather, spoken to him as well." He looked back at the men, then at her again. "You will do this, not knowing what sort of person she is, whether or not she can help you. You wish to put yourself up for her and help her?"

"We do. If you can allow it. I don't want to break any of your rules, nor do I wish to step on your toes in this. I understand more than most what it is to be in charge and have someone try to undermine your authority." He nodded. "She'll be welcome in our home, no matter if she can work or not."

"Noreen is a good woman. She often helps with the galas and meetings that we have. She is an excellent cook, and sadly has had to deal with these boys for a very long time on her own. Their father, he's the one that will be blamed for today. I shall take care of him as well. But the mother...as you said, it has been difficult for her to have such idiots as sons." Evan came to stand next to her as Nathan continued. "I will allow her to come to your home, if she wishes it. I think, after this, she will wash her hands of the family that she has tried so hard to keep together. Some people, it seems, have no wish to better themselves."

"Thank you, Nathan. You're a good leader." Evan looked at the young men when Nathan did. Then he spoke to him again. "I have a feeling that they were only following the direction of their older brother. Not that it excuses what they've done, but as soon as you contacted them, they dropped their weapons and stopped. The only one that didn't was James, and he's dead because of it. Should you like to let them work off their

160

punishment after jail, I'd gladly help you with that."

"You're a good man as well, Evan. Thank you." The young men were arrested and taken away. Nathan looked at them before continuing. "I should warn you that in two weeks I'll be stepping down as pack leader. My son, Nate, he'll be running things. He will have me to help him should he need it, but I think he'll do very well. Today just underlines the fact that I'm too old for this shit. A younger man needs to be in charge."

"I'm sure that he will. I look forward to working with him. And you as well."

After they were released, Evan took Dylan's hand and nearly dragged her to the car. He never said a word, but as soon as they were at the house, he turned to look at her.

"Run."

Getting out of the car, she took off to the woods. She had a feeling that when he caught her, she was going to pay for getting hurt today. And she was as excited as she was aroused.

CHAPTER 12

David loved doing research, but this was particularly fun. He'd been finding things out about his brother's home for a week now, and knew as much about the house as he did his family. Evan and Dylan had a better home than anyone would have ever guessed. He couldn't wait to tell them about it.

"You looked pleased." He told his dad that he was. "I heard that you were working on something for Evan. You about done with it, or you got a bit more? I was hoping I could bend your ear for a little while."

"Nearly done. I think I'm going to write a book about the house, if he doesn't mind. There is a lot of rich history about the house and the people that lived and worked there. I have a meeting with him for dinner." Dad nodded. "You okay? I thought you and Mom were going to take a trip to Denver for a few days."

"She's got this thing with the historical women going now, and she'd not got the time to go. I was kinda hoping you and I could hang out together. Don't see you as much as we used to. You still selling them books pretty good?" He told Dad that he was selling well. "I would have guessed that you would. I don't know where you get that talent, but I sure am proud of you."

"Thanks, Dad. I'm sorry Mom is so busy. I know you were looking forward to getting away for a little while." He said it was fine, and picked up one of the numerous pictures he'd unearthed. "Those were found in one of the cabinets in the rooms you found. There are a great many of them that are marked with dates and names, but a lot that aren't. I've been trying to piece them together with the faces that I know."

"This is Miss Ester McFarland if I don't miss my bet. Her family...let me see. Her family has been around here as long as we have, more maybe. They owned a lot of property around here before the town came in. I think they might have been the ones that sold off the property that the courthouse sits on. She lived in that house about the time that these photos were taken." He handed him the one that he'd been working on, where the same woman sat in the chair alongside of a big man. "That's her, sitting there with her ankles showing. That was frowned upon back then, but you can tell she don't give a lick of care about it."

"Is this her family?" Dad nodded and said he didn't know all their names. "Any of them would help. What was her husband's name?"

"I don't think she ever married him." Dad laughed hard. "She was a rebel. And during that time, it was frowned upon to be shacked up with someone, even if you had a bunch of kiddies. His name was Harold Decker. Nice man. He took really good care of her and that brood of hers. I don't know that the two of them had any together, but she had a couple and they took in a few more before he passed."

"Dad, she called the house Decker House. Did you know

that?" He said that he might have a while back, but had forgotten. "The house was also used as part of the Underground Railroad for a while. I found records dating back to 1820."

"That's about right, I think. You want some help here?" David said he'd love some. "Good. I got nothing else going on with all the hay in and the others working the ranch. Did I tell you that I got a broodmare coming in? She's a beauty. I'm gonna breed her with Siam."

They talked about the ranch and the pictures for nearly three hours. When his dad said he was going to order some dinner, David suggested that they go and have a meal together. Dad asked if the others might come along.

"I'd love that. I know that Evan is home today. I spoke to him a few hours ago, right around noon. Joshua had a house to show, but he's surely done with that now. Adam and Blake are coming in tonight to have a little fun, and Adrian is buried to his eyes in legal work for his upcoming election."

"I'm so proud of you boys that I could about bust. To think when you guys started coming along, all I could think about was how to feed you. Even back then you would eat more than I thought humanly possible." David told him that he loved him. "I love you too, son. All of you just are the best thing to me and your momma."

David called his brothers and told them to meet him and dad at the Warehouse. They served a great steak dinner and the best iced tea. Even before the rest of them showed up, he decided to invite Norris and Bailey. They might as well make a big family showing, he thought.

They were well into dinner when Dad brought up the house. Passing around the pictures, hoping for some other input on the people in them, he was startled when Bailey started naming people he knew.

"I remember Miss McFarland. Her and her family was about as rich as they come, even back then." He laid down the picture and picked up the one of mostly children and her sitting in the middle. "She'd take in just about anybody that made it to her home. One time my daddy was cutting her yard for her, and she had about fifty people working in the household. Too many for such a house, but they were all polishing silver and doing chores. Daddy told me once that he thought she was touched in the head, but I thought she was about the nicest woman ever. She'd make me fried pies when I'd come with Daddy to work."

"Bailey, did she ever marry Decker?" His grandpa was helping Bailey along with his memories. Grandpa talked about the mister. "I remember old Harold. He was a tall drink of water, and quiet. I suppose that when you had a woman that never shut up, you'd learn to be quiet. But he sure did love that woman."

"She sure did talk, and she was never one to let an opinion she had go unnoticed. I think she's the one that told Daddy I'd be worth something someday." Bailey looked so sad. "I guess she was wrong about that part."

"Oh, pshaw, Bailey." Dad looked around the table, then back at the man as he continued. "You come in here and tell us things we didn't know, and that makes you worthy in my book. Why, David is gonna write a book about the place. Your help will make his facts so much nicer."

Bailey smiled then. "When I was about ten or so, I remember someone saying that the family had worked with the Underground. I was a might confused, wondering if she was working in the graveyard. So, I went to ask her about it, just to see if she saw any bodies." Bailey laughed. "She told me that she and her family had been helpful in getting a lot of families out of the country when it was in a bad way. And that some of those people they helped would have been in deep trouble had their masters found them."

"She must have been old even then, I'm thinking." Bailey said he thought she'd been born old, and they all laughed. "You're a lucky man to have gotten to talk to her like that. Most were terrified of her."

"She knew that, I think…what the town and the people thought of her. I don't think she cared all that much. Even when I was a little boy, she would wonder where that story came from." David asked if he knew how old she was. "Yes, sir. And if you'd like, I can give you her Bible and her working book. She gave them to me."

David was stunned to silence. A family Bible would mean not only would he have births and deaths of the family, but marriages as well as numerous other things. When Bailey told him he could come by and get them anytime, Norris asked him where they were, in case he wasn't there when David came by.

"In my chest. There's pictures in there too. And some things of your momma's. You should take it all, son, to do with what you want." Norris said he'd do that, and looked at David when his dad did. "I have a lot of things you might find interesting, young man. I'm clear as a bell right now, so I'll tell you where they are. I got a safety deposit box in the bank. Number forty-four. The keys are in the chest, and I'm telling you now so that Norris can take you by to get it. I think it's all right there. The bank has been holding it for me for nearly fifty years now."

167

"Thank you, Bailey. You don't know how much I appreciate you letting me use these things." He told him to do with them what he wanted, they were his. "I can't thank you enough. When I've gotten all I can from them, I'll give them to my mom. One of her organizations is opening the historical society again in a few weeks."

Bailey nodded and sat and watched them the rest of the night. No matter how many times David tried to get him engaged again, Bailey seemed to be content with just listening. He looked exhausted tonight, he thought. Like he was having trouble staying awake. It was sad to him. David really liked the older gentleman.

David decided right then that he was going to dedicate the book to the man. He had been, in just an hour, more helpful than anyone else had. He couldn't wait to see what treasures there were in the bank and the chest.

"Might not be much at all," Norris told him later. "I mean, there is a chest and it's his, but as far as what's in it, who knows? My dad was ill before my mom passed, and he's not any better now about remembering. It might be filled with matchbooks for all I know. He's very protective of it. I was surprised when he offered to give it to you. But don't get your hopes up of it being very helpful."

"I don't mind, Norris. The little that he gave us here, that's going to go a long way in getting in touch with some of the people that worked in the big house." Norris told him again not to expect too much. "I won't. But every part of it will be a gift."

They were going to meet in the morning at the bank, Norris bringing the keys with him to open the safety deposit box, then they were going back to the house for the chest. As they were telling everyone goodbye, David thanked Bailey again.

"You do right by those people, okay?" He said he would. "I liked that old woman. She was a nice person. If you find out something bad, don't tell me. I got a picture of her in my heart that I don't want to tarnish."

"I won't, Bailey. I'll make sure she continues to be a good person to everyone that knew her." He hugged him then. Bailey held him tightly in his arms, and David felt his eyes fill with tears.

The man had lost the best part of him, but when he was able, he showed parts of his true self, and David loved it. As he made his way home, he was already working on the dedication page for all the help he'd gotten.

~~~

Dylan laid the phone down on the desk she was sitting at. No words could have prepared her for the grief she was feeling right now. Her grandda had died.

"You all right?" She shook her head at Eve. "What is it, child? Tell me. Is your family all right? Do they need you?"

"My grandda died last night." Eve came to her then, pulled her up from the chair and just held her. Sobbing out the rest of the story, she told her that her mom had found him when he'd not come down to breakfast. "She said he just went to sleep and didn't wake up. What am I going to do without him around?"

"He'd have wanted you to go on. Oh sweetheart, I'm so sorry for your loss. He was such a wonderful man." She nodded and cried harder. "Is your momma all right? Does she need for you to come home?"

"She said that Dad is there with her and that he's pretty upset. The hospital is on the way there to get him. He was my rock. And such a wonderful man." Eve held her tighter as she cried. "Every time I'd get the chance to call home, he'd tell me the same stories. How he'd gotten in trouble with the law. Of course he hadn't, but he loved telling me that. Then he'd go on with this elaborate tale about how he'd had to beat off ten men to get the roses that he put on Grandma's grave. That he'd had to go without food for four days, always four, to buy them for her."

"He was a very special man, your grandfather. I loved being able to spend some time with him, getting to know him. Bailey was a good man." Dylan thought of the stories that Evan had told her last night. How much fun her grandda had had. Even how clear he'd been when talking to them about the pictures.

"What am I going to do without him?" Eve sat down in front of her and held her hand. "He is with Grandma now, isn't he?"

"I'm sure he's up there looking down on us right now, wondering what all the fuss is about. He lived a good life, child. And now that he's with your grandma, you can bet he's telling her a whale of a tale as well." Dylan nodded and laughed a little. "He helped David with his story, did he tell you? David said that it was like sitting down with a history book, all the things he'd told him."

"David told my dad last night that he was going to dedicate the book to him. He asked Dad his full name so that he'd get it right."

Eve sat with her until she was feeling better. Evan had been in town all day with his patients. He called her several times, telling her how much he loved her and how sorry he was. She was just glad that Grandda's last night on this earth was spent with family and friends.

Evan called her about an hour later, telling her that he was finishing up. She was done crying, or she'd thought so, and talking to him hurt her all over. Dylan told him that his mom had been with her today, and that they'd gotten some of the boxes packed up.

"Good. I was wondering when I'd get around to that. Its fall season in the hospital, and there seems to be a lot more accidents than usual. I think its people just having their minds on other things like the holidays, and not paying attention." She asked him if his surgeries went well. "They did. I had three early this morning, and one assist. It's tiring, but I feel good when I can make someone better. I have an appointment with the head of the department in about a half hour. I'm not looking forward to that."

"Maybe he wants you to be the head of surgical. You said there was an opening." He told her that he thought they were going outside the department to fill that position. "It would be a shame. They have you right there and you're good."

"You only think I'm good because you love me. For all you know I could be a major flop. I'll be home in a couple of hours. How about you and I go into town and be with your mom and dad?" She told him that her dad wanted to be alone and that mom was too upset to entertain. "Then we'll go to the house and see how much progress they made today. I was told that we have a kitchen."

"I'd like to move in as soon as we can. Do you think that the bedrooms will be done enough that we can use them? I just want to be with you." He said they'd check on that as well. "All right, but I'm going to shower and change. I'll see you when you get here."

After hanging up with him, she wandered into the backyard. It was so lovely here at his parents', but she wanted to be somewhere she could be alone. It wasn't often that she felt this way, but it had been a difficult morning. She'd not realized how much she depended on Evan to keep her steady all the time.

Blake joined her just as she sat down. Dylan wanted to tell him to go away, but he smiled at her and asked her if she was busy. Shaking her head, she nodded and stood up.

"I was hoping you would help me out. Can you come to the ranch with me?" She told him she wasn't in the mood to be with anyone right now. "Neither am I. I prefer my own company to that of people, even shifters. But I have a calf that needs some help, and I'm well into prepping the tractors for winter."

She followed him to the barn. "Is this a ploy to get me out of my funk? It won't work, I can tell you that right now."

"Probably not. I heard about your grandda, and I'm so sorry. I don't know what I'd do if mine were to leave me. But I really do need your help. I'd ask one of my brothers, but they're all busy. This time of year, it's tough putting our big boy toys away." She smiled when he laughed. "This is Winnie. Her momma, sadly, didn't make it through birth. It happens sometimes, and no matter what we do, we lose one or two. But Winnie is starving and won't let me touch her."

"Because you're a cat." Blake shook his head. "Then why won't she let you.... She thinks you killed her mom?"

"No. Good heavens no. She's afraid of me. I might have gone a little.... Well, I hate to lose one, and I was pretty pissed. I didn't hurt her, but she heard me cursing. Animals are very sensitive about things like that." She didn't believe him, but when he walked to the small calf, she ran away from him and cowered in the corner. "See? She's upset about something I did. Could you feed her?"

"Feed her? I'm not sure you noticed, but neither am I a cow, thank you very much, nor am I lactating. You'll have to think of something else." His face turned the brightest shade of red she'd ever seen. And even apologizing didn't make it lessen. "I was kidding you, Blake. Just tell me what you want me to do."

"A bottle. I have...I'm so sorry. I meant for you to come out and give her a bottle." Nodding, she just couldn't look at him. He was falling all over himself trying to make up for calling her...well, she supposed he'd called her a cow, but he was fine and so was she.

The bottle was as big as her arm. And thick too. The nipple alone looked like she could wear it on her head. And once he told her what to do, how to hold it, the baby just latched on like it was hungry.

"Are you going to be all right doing this? I really need to get some work done today." She told him she was fine after getting instructions on how much to feed Winnie. "Just let her roam around in here, or you can take her into the paddock. But I can't tell you how much I appreciate this."

When he left her, she watched Winnie eat. It was funny how she looked like someone had taken an adult cow and shrunk it in the dryer. All except for the ears. She had the biggest ones she'd ever seen on an animal.

"You're very messy, anyone ever tell you that?" Winnie just watched her as she drank down her breakfast. "I'm sorry about your momma. I lost someone today too. My grandda. He would have loved feeding you."

Drool dripped off her mouth and onto the ground. She wondered if she might need a bib, and laughed a little. Dylan knew nothing about cows and such, but she was enjoying this part of it. Blake had told her that in a few days she'd get used to all of them, but right now she was scared and lonely.

"I'm lonely too, you know. Maybe I'll come out here and we can talk about our losses together." Winnie just watched her with those big cow eyes. "What happens to you now? I mean, yes, they want you to get healthy, but does that mean that I'm fattening you up for dinner one night?"

"She's a milker." Startled, she stepped in front of the calf and drew her gun. It took her frightened mind a few seconds to realize it was Oliver. If he was nervous, he didn't show it. "Blake said you were helping him out. Thank you. I have a bit of work I'm taking care of too."

"He said her momma died." Oliver nodded as he moved to the stall beside her. "I was only making small talk with her. I feel sort of silly now."

"Don't be. I talk to the corn and hay we grow too. It's a way to pass the time." She nodded, and when the bottle was empty, Winnie fussed at her. "If you want to give her another bottle, I can make it up for you. She's not had anything for a few hours, and I would think she could use a little extra."

Dylan nodded. "I'm sorry that you lost one of your cows. That must hit you hard too." He said it did. "I've never been this close to a cow before. I mean, sometimes we'd see them when we were out on a mission, but we never got close enough to touch them."

"I've been giving it some thought about you and your

174

missions. If you don't mind, I'd like to ask you a couple questions." She told him sure as she took the bottle back to Winnie. "I'm wondering, as a woman, if you had any trouble from those that worked under you. And if you knew if you had any shifters in your group."

"Some trouble being a woman, but not so much from the men I worked with. Mostly it was the other countries. I remember once getting stoned by a few men that thought I should have been home baking. Then another time they decided to make me a poster girl for what happens to women who think they're better than a man. That didn't end well for them." He smiled. "And yes, I worked with a great many shifters. There were some on my team."

"I thought so. You didn't seem all that surprised when you found out that Evan was one. Were they helpful to you? I mean, in the setting you were in?" She told him that they'd shift and go ahead of the team and relay back what was going on. "I can see that would be very helpful."

He was getting to something, she knew it, but decided rather than make him get to the point, she'd let him do it at his own pace. Winnie finished up her lunch and wandered into the paddock. Dylan watched her from the barn doors.

"Dylan, I was wondering if I could talk to you about a woman in the leap." She told him that he could talk to her about anything. "She's with a man that hurts her. I'd like for you to teach her to fight back. If you could."

"Is it her mate?" Oliver shook his head. "All right, I can do that. Are you talking fists or guns too, Oliver? Either one will keep her safe, but the gun is much faster."

"Fists for now. This man, he thinks because he's bigger than her and she needs his income that he can teach her lessons. I don't care for his lesson plan, nor him." She nodded and asked him why he'd not done it. "Because I'd just kill him."

CHAPTER 13

Annie saw the woman, but went about hanging the laundry on the line. There was something so calming about seeing sheets hanging in the breeze. When she was finished with the last one, she bent to pick up the basket and cried out in pain. Her back was hurting her something terrible.

"I have that." The woman took the basket and held it in front of her. Annie was afraid that Eddy would see her talking to someone. "He's on the Whitfield ranch today. Oliver needed some extra help and he was made to go. Oliver wanted me to see you."

"Oliver sent you?" She nodded. "I don't know why he'd do something like that. I'm not doing nothing wrong."

"No. What's being done wrong is against you, not by you." Annie looked around again. She knew that Eddy had spies. "No one is going to tell him either. I've taken care of that myself."

"What do you mean? I'd like for you to go now." Instead of going back the way she'd come, the woman went to the back door of her home and went inside. Her children were in there the way that Eddy had left them, and she was afraid for them. She was bent over Charlie when Annie walked in. "Don't touch her. You can't let her go or there will be hell to pay."

"I'm going to free you all if you'll let me." Annie felt hope leap into her heart. Then it was gone just as quickly. "My name is Dylan Whitfield. I'm mate to Evan."

"Evan is a good man." She looked at her children, free now but still huddled in the corner like they were still tied. "Eddy hates them. He thinks that I should drown them, and he's cruel to us."

"That's what I heard. Oliver sent me to help you, but I think this goes beyond you being able to defend yourself, doesn't it? You're here because of your children." Annie nodded, her heart breaking at someone knowing about her life. "I'm going to take you to my house and we're going to—"

"You can't. He'll kill them and me." Dylan said he'd never get the chance. "You don't know him. He's a mean man. Nasty to those that try and tell him anything. When my mate was alive, he'd not even let him into our home. But now that Charles is gone, Eddy's here all the time, moving in and taking over. Eddy is the leap leader now."

"Since when?" Annie told her since Wednesday. "I hadn't heard about that. I don't think any of the Whitfields have either."

"We're forbidden. He said that if anyone other than the encampment knew that he'd kill them and every one of us. He can if we disobey him." Dylan stood up and looked around the house. Annie went with her, pointing out some of the *improvements* that Eddy had made since he'd moved in. She'd already signed her death warrant, she figured, by talking to her, so Dylan might as well have it all.

"He keeps the children tied up like that all the time?" She

told her that he threw scraps of food at them like they were animals too. "And you? Where does he keep you when he's gone?"

"I had to do his wash." Dylan asked her again. "In the shed. Sometimes I'm out there for several days before he releases me. Last week...last week I was out there for five days without food or water. When he finds out that I've talked to you, he'll kill me this time. Would you please...? I want you to take my children with you when you leave here. I need to know that they're safe."

"Evan and Oliver are coming to help you move." She shook her head. "Listen to me. If you stay, he'll kill you. If the children stay, he'll kill them first while you watch, and then kill you. Do you want that to happen?"

"He'll come after us." Dylan said good. "No, you don't understand. He's a monster. He'll hurt you."

"No, he'll try and hurt me, but it won't work. I'm smarter and prettier." She laughed. Annie hadn't laughed out loud in a good long time, and it felt good. "Good for you. Now, pack what you think you need, and they'll load you up and take you somewhere safe."

Charlie was the first to get moving. Within ten minutes she had her brother, Shawn, cleaned up and his things packed. It was a pitifully small number of things. It had been so long since her children had had anything. Eddy had burned all their toys a few months ago, when he was pissed that she'd not had steaks to feed him and his buddies.

Evan had brought his medical bag with him and checked out the children. Charlie had a burn on her back that Eddy had given her when he'd decided to brand her. And Shawn was fighting a terrible cold.

"They're malnourished as well as dehydrated. When we get you settled in the house, we'll make sure that they have plenty to eat and some medicine for Shawn." She nodded. "Now, I'm going to check out your wounds. How long has he been using you for a punching bag?"

"Eight months, nine days, and sixteen hours." He stared at her for several seconds. "My husband...I think Eddy killed him to hurt me, and that's how long my Charles has been gone."

"I'm sorry that this has happened to you." She nodded, tears flowing freely now. It had been so long, it seemed, since anyone had been kind to her. "Dylan and I are going to take you home with us. The kids too. My dad and mom are going to keep them for a few days while you are hospitalized. I'm concerned about your back injury."

"He beat me with a belt, and when that didn't do whatever it was he wanted, he'd use the poker from the fireplace." She cried harder when he hugged her to him. Annie knew that Eddy was going to smell the other man on her, but she needed this more than she thought possible.

The children were on an adventure. They were very quiet, but she could see hope in their eyes that they might be safe. Charlie promised her several times that she'd be well behaved and that she'd take care of Shawn. Annie knew this. When she was put into the big truck that was going to take her to the hospital, she thought of what she was leaving behind.

Memories of her late husband. The children's pictures and clothing. Things they'd made for her. Books that they treasured, and her mom's cookbook. Things that would surely be destroyed as soon as Eddy came back and saw they were all gone, and when he smelled the Whitfields on the things that they'd touched. She hoped that he'd never find them.

Annie knew it was going to be terrible. He'd come for her and kill her children if given the chance. But she also knew, as others did, that the Whitfields were not ones to mess with. She thought secretly that was why Eddy had not wanted them to know that he'd killed the leap leader. He was afraid they'd come and ask questions. She had a few herself.

Had Eddy killed Charles? She was sure that he had. As surely as she was alive, she thought that. Eddy hated them, and especially Charles. And when he'd been found, his neck broken and his body beaten, her first thought was that he'd killed her love. Then he'd forced his way into her home and had raped her repeatedly while the children were in the other room. It had been that way for months now, and she was sure that his plan was to kill her slowly.

"I want you to be here for a couple of days, Annie." She nodded at Evan when he came into her hospital room. "There are guards outside of your room, and no one will be able to come in unless I approve of them. Also, I want you to know that your children are safe and guarded as well. I need for you to get well, and worrying won't help. I'm trying to get in touch with Darryl."

"He's the leader. I mean, Eddy is now." Evan said nothing, but she could see the shock on his face. "He killed Darryl White, but we weren't to tell you, or anyone that doesn't live in the encampment, for fear of death. I don't know how he did it, but he declared himself leap leader and killed his family. The children weren't there. I'm not sure where they are, but he couldn't find them."

"I'll figure this out." She nodded. "Annie, do you think he

killed Charles? I mean, I'm not asking you to say for sure, but you think he did?"

"Yes, with all my heart." He nodded, then stood and went to the door. "Evan, promise me that you're going to protect my children from him. I don't know what I would do if he harmed them."

"He'll never touch any of you again." It was said with so much conviction that she believed him. "You just listen to what we tell you and you'll be fine. But I promise you, he'll never hurt any of you again."

Rolling to her side, she shivered. Eddy was going to be in a world of hurt, she thought, if he did come after them. Smiling, she closed her eyes. She wished she could be there when Evan took him on. Annie was sure it was going to be a fight to end all, and hopefully Eddy.

~~~

Eddy Finley was bone tired. He'd never worked this hard in his life. And the fact that the old man working him stood nearby so that he'd not be able to fuck off pissed him off even more. As soon as he was able to tell them he was their leader, he was going to kill all the Whitfields and have their guts hung from a tree. Fucking dicks.

When he entered the house, the first thing he smelled was another tiger. He sniffed deeper as he walked around the living room, and thought that the smell was familiar but wasn't sure from where. He looked to where the kids were supposed to be and was pissed that the rope he'd used was cut. The fucking cunt was going to pay for this.

"Annie? Where the fuck are those brats?" Nothing. He thought that he'd let her out of the shed this morning to do wash, but couldn't remember. Going there now, he saw that the door was wide open and there was wash on the line. Fucking bitch was going to be sorry for disobeying him.

There were things missing besides his family. The stacked up pile of clothing that the kids had was gone. Their jackets and book bags as well. The things in the kitchen, the items that he'd been saving to break for a special occasion, were gone too. The flower vase that had been ugly. The books that Annie treasured. Even a few of the knives that he'd threatened and sometimes cut her with were missing. Going to the basement, he knew that's where he'd find them all.

"Annie, this is not going to go well for you if you don't come on out now. I might even be persuaded to not kill the kids if you give me yourself for an hour. I can hurt you really bad in that much time." The woman came out of the shadows and he took a step back from her. "Who the fuck are you?"

"Dylan." Like that was supposed to help him. "They're not here. Annie and her children are safe and being taken care of. You should know better than to hurt someone smaller than you. I'm here to make sure that you learn that lesson first. Then I'm going to kill your ass."

"You think you can tell me what to do? Well I got news for you, bitch, I'm not easily scared off. You go and get Annie right now and I won't hurt you while I'm teaching her a lesson." She laughed. "You won't think this is so funny if I hit you."

"Give it your best shot." He felt fear, just a small finger of it, run down his spine. But she laughed again and he wanted to hit her in the worst kind of way. "Come on, Eddy boy. Are you afraid of little old me? You should be, just so you know."

He drew back his fist to hit her, and found himself on the

floor with his arm up behind his back. It was fucking painful, and the harder he struggled to get loose, the more she pulled his arm. Then it popped and he was dizzy with the pain.

"Do you know who I am? I'm the leap leader. I'm going to have you killed. And I can too, bitch. Just on my say so, I can have the entire leap tearing you apart." Her laughter was getting on his nerves. "You won't think this is so funny when I get up from here."

"I think I will, but then you don't strike me as having a very good sense of humor. Nor very much in the brain pan. What am I supposed to do when you tell me that you're the leap leader anyway? Tremble in my boots? Or do you expect me to wet my panties in fear? I'm not going to do any of those, in case you were wondering. I can hurt you in so many ways, you'll beg me to kill you."

He was pretty sure that she thought she was right, but he was bigger than her and he wasn't stupid. When he tried to move out from under her, he was freed. Eddy was sure that she'd let him go, but wasn't going to ask her. Standing in front of her, he could see that she thought she was all tough and stuff, but she wasn't anything but a human. He could kill her by just shifting and letting his cat have at her.

"You should know a couple of things before you do something...well, something else stupid. I'm Dylan Whitfield. Mate to Evan Whitfield. And he's upstairs now gathering more of the things that Annie left behind." His balls actually curled up closer to his body. His cat, usually so aggressive, whimpered to him and moved away. "I can see by the expression on your face that you're well aware of who he is."

"You're lying." She just shrugged, something that he'd

hated to have people do to him since he'd been a little cub. "I'm going to kill you, bitch."

"Bitch. You've called me that several times now. Don't you know any other words? I do. Let me think. Bitch. Okay. Cunt. Wait, you used that one too. Harpy? How about shrew? Dog? No, that one doesn't make me think of an insult. There's she-devil." He told her to shut up. "You're not very nice, are you? Well, neither am I. Hello, Evan."

He turned and saw the man sitting on the step. Evan was a big man, strong too from the stories he'd heard, and Eddy was terrified of him finding him. When he blew kisses at Dylan, Eddy found himself dodging them, like they were going to hurt him.

"Hello, Eddy. You should know that I've talked to the council about your behavior. And they're going to talk to you soon. If you're still alive." He asked if Evan was going to kill him. "No, I'm not."

Relief was profound. When he looked at Dylan again, she laughed. There was something about her laughter that made him afraid this time. When she stretched her body, he noticed the gun in the top of her pants. The knife in her pocket. He looked at Evan again.

"I'm not going to kill you. She is." Eddy thought he'd heard him wrong. There was no way he was going to let his mate do this. And her being only a human? Maybe he wanted him to kill her. That was it. "Darling, I'm going to finish up with the things upstairs. When you're finished, we'll head home. The bedrooms are complete enough that we can stay in them tonight."

Then he stood up and left them down there. Dylan took out her gun and put it on the shelf beside her. Then the knives.

There were four of them, all silver, and they looked to be as sharp as her tongue. When she asked him how he wanted this to go, he had no idea what she was talking about.

"Do you want to die quickly or slowly? I'm hoping for slow, but you're a big pussy that beats defenseless children, so that might not be very much fun for me either." He told her he was her leader. "Not mine, you're not. A leader doesn't beat children. Doesn't kill a man just to torture his wife and kids. You are so not a leader. An asshole, yes, but never a leader. You're a bully and a prick."

"How did you find out?" She just shrugged. "You do that again and I'm going to kill you. That is the rudest thing a person could do."

She stared at him for several seconds before bursting out laughing. "You think that is the only rude thing going on around here? Me shrugging at you? You mother fucker, you killed two men that I know of, and then tied children to a hook in the floor. What do you call that if not rude?" He told her that they were lucky that he'd kept them alive. "No, that would be you that is lucky to be alive. Had I been in Annie's situation, I would have cut your little dick off and made you eat the thing. I still might do that."

"If you hurt me, I'll turn you over to the council." He was reaching for anything now. He'd already been told that they were after him. But she shrugged again and he leapt at her. "I'm not kidding, bitch. When I come after you, you're going to know what pain is really like."

She moved just as he shifted. His cat hit the wall behind her and hit his head. Eddy turned to her, his claws out and ready, when he noticed that in her hurry to get away from him, she'd

186

left her weapons. This was going to be much easier than he'd thought.

The second time he lunged at her, she laughed. Sidestepping him was quick…her body wasn't even touched by his bigger one. And when she hit him in the ribs with her fist, his cat snarled at her and the fucking bitch slapped him on the nose.

"I've heard that it's incredibly painful to be slapped like that. Maybe you like pain, but I'm thinking that is only because you've not felt enough of it. My kind of pain. If you come at me again, I'm going to seriously hurt you."

He lunged again, his feet hitting her solid in the chest even as the pain in his head exploded. Falling to the floor, he smelled his own blood. Looking to see what sort of damage he'd done to her, he saw that she was unharmed, her body intact. By the way he'd hit her, she should have been dead. He snarled at her again.

"Is that all you have, Eddy boy? You're not all that much, are you?" She started to circle him as he did the same to her. "Are you getting tired of this little game? I am. You should know that the next time you come at me, you'll be dead. I'm sick of fucking with you."

He'd attacked her three times now, and she was none the worse for wear. Eddy tried to think what he was doing wrong. How he was letting a mere human female beat him. When she paused by the table where her weapons were, he noticed that she didn't even look, but picked up the knife that was laying with the others. It was time to end this.

Snapping his teeth at her made her jump back. It was what he'd hoped for when he jumped at her again. It was going to be as easy as beating one of the kids, taking her down. But he hadn't counted on her being quick. Nor her obvious training with the weapons.

The knife entered his body, but he was sure that he'd hurt her, and dropping to the floor to shift, he had to catch his breath before he could move. Eddy looked at the woman.

She had a bloody nose and nothing more. Not a hair on her head was mussed up, nor did she look like she hurt. He did. Looking at his shoulder, he could see the blade was still there, the silver of it making him slightly dizzy.

"You ready to give up?" He snarled at her. "I'm taking that as a no. Damn it man, do you want me to kill you? This shit was easier when I was able to just shoot first and never ask questions. But they want you to suffer."

He couldn't ask her who she was talking about, but she seemed to understand. Calling for Evan, the man came back to the stairs and sat down. Dylan asked him what he was saying.

Speaking to the other tiger made him realize that he'd been right about Evan. The man was leap leader material. They'd never exchanged blood so they shouldn't have been able to talk. Eddy thought maybe he might have bitten off more than he could chew with this woman. He asked Evan who wanted him to suffer.

"Other than Annie? Well, there would be the council, plus Darryl's children. And the four or five others that we're still trying to find. You were sloppy, Eddy. And now you're going to pay for that."

Eddy asked him why he wasn't down here. Why he was being a pussy and letting his mate be the one that suffered. Evan laughed and stood again. He winked at his mate before turning to the door again.

"Because she'll make a better leap leader than anyone I know." He felt his skin crawl, and his cat whimper again. "Kill him, Dylan. I want to go home."

He looked at the woman again and she was holding her gun. Eddy knew that she'd not shoot him, that he'd be able to talk her out of it. But when she shrugged again, he felt his anger take him, then nothing as the sound of the gun firing filled his head.

CHAPTER 14

Evan woke to the most amazing sensation. As soon as he opened his eyes, he knew that it wasn't a dream but the best reality that he'd ever experienced...seeing Dylan atop him, giving herself pleasure as she cupped her breasts and tugged at her nipples.

"Can I join you?" Her moan was almost too much. "Christ, love. You're beautiful. Let me take you."

"No, please, not yet. I'm having fun." Her hips rolling over his, she leaned down and kissed him hungrily. "I woke up and thought that I should start my day. And what better way than having you inside of me."

Evan put his hands on her hips, trying to slow her a little so he could catch up with her. She was beautiful, sexy, and loving too. As she moaned louder, her hand holding him while she played with her nipples, all he could think about was fucking her hard. Taking her so deeply that she screamed out his name.

"Evan, now. Make me come." Rolling her to her back, he slid over her. Her legs wrapped around his, her hands tangled in his hair. When she bowed up, her body pressed hard into his, he felt her tighten around him, her sheath milk him tightly.

It was all it took to bring him with her. Crying out his own release, he bit down on her throat when she offered it to him.

He came twice. Not that it was unusual for him with her, but they were hard, mind numbing releases that made him feel like he was going to pass out. And when Dylan dug her nails into his back, he saw stars. Colorful ones that were moving at dizzying speeds. Then he dropped onto her, no longer able to hold himself upright.

The next time he opened his eyes he was alone in the bed. The light was shining brightly in the room, and he decided that curtains would need to be purchased if he was going to need to rest up during the day. Going into the bathroom, he found a note on the counter and read it while the water warmed up for his shower.

"I'm at the store with Noreen. I've never shopped for food before, so this might be an experience for both of us. She's wonderful, by the way, and I'm glad that she's working for us. Also, before I forget, we have a meeting with the council tonight. I'm sure that they're going to kick my ass for killing that prick." Then it was signed, Dylan.

He stepped under the spray as he thought about the death of Eddy. And how for the first time since becoming a doctor he was feeling good about the death of a person. Justified, as a matter of fact.

Evan had been at his parents' house the day before he'd been killed, and the children, Charlie and Shawn, were having breakfast. Well, they were staring at the plates and not touching them. He asked his mom what was going on and noticed that she had been crying.

"What is it?" She nodded to the children and he switched to talking to her on their link. *What is wrong, Mom? Did they say something to you?*

Yes, he starved them. He told her that he'd heard that too. *No, you don't understand. He starved them of even the basic things like human contact. Love, even a kind word. Do you know why they're not eating? They're waiting for him to come in the door and hit them. Which he did all the time, Evan.*

He sat with the children while his mom made him something to eat as well. Evan had eaten at the hospital before coming here, but he thought it would be good for them to see him having the meal as well.

"I'd like to talk to you both." Charlie was very protective of her brother and put her hand on his shoulder. "I won't hurt you. You know that, don't you?"

"No, we don't know anything about you." He nodded and poured syrup over his pancakes. "Where did you take our momma?"

"She's in the hospital. I was going to release her this afternoon, but if you want, I can take you in to see her." Charlie nodded. "Eddy is going to pay for what he's done to you guys and her."

"We heard that before." He nodded and helped Shawn cut his pancakes up. Evan wasn't sure what Charlie thought was going to happen, but she backed from him as far as she could go. "They told us that he was a mean man and that he hurt others."

"He did. Eddy hurt a great many people." She nodded and picked up her fork and played with the pancakes. "Mom can make you eggs if you want. I'm a waffle man myself, but she's so happy to have you two here that she'd make you just about anything."

"Will you have sex with us too?" Evan nearly cut his hand when Shawn said that. His voice was low, as if he were terrified of the answer. Evan didn't even look at his mom. "I don't want to. It hurts and I can't go to the bathroom no more."

His hands were shaking when he picked up his fork. Anger was making his beast snarl and snap inside of him. When his mom came and touched her hand to his shoulder, he wanted to hide his face in her bosom and let her make it all go away. Instead, he looked at Charlie.

"Did he have sex with you both?" She nodded, but didn't look at him. "Did your momma know?"

"No. He said if we told her, he'd kill us all." Evan then looked at his mom and she shook her head, telling him, he supposed, that she'd not known that either. "Will you?"

"No, not ever. And no one else will either until you're old enough to say it's okay." She nodded and continued to play with her food. "Charlie, look at me."

When she did, he saw her sadness. The look of defeat on her face. Shawn had it as well, but he had fear too. He started to touch her but she jerked back from him. Evan wanted to pick them both up and hold them until they believed it was going to be all right again.

"I'm going to talk to him today. Dylan and I will." She nodded. "And when we're done, you won't ever have to worry about him again. I swear to you on my mother's heart, he will never hurt you or anyone again."

Charlie looked at him. Her eyes narrowed to slits as it felt to him that she was sizing him up. The next words out of her mouth had shaken him to his very core. And it was what made him able to tell Dylan to kill the man.

"The only way to get rid of a mad dog is to put a bullet in his head. He'll come back if you don't. My daddy used to say that." Evan told her he understood. "My momma is sad, Mr. Evan. If you take care of him, she might smile again."

"I promise you that we'll take care of him." She nodded. "But you have to do something for me. You have to get well. Eat when you're hungry, and tell people, anyone, when you're afraid. I'll make sure that you have my numbers when you and your mom leave here. All right?"

All that day he was riddled with the thought of that monster hurting these children in such a way that.... Well, Evan would have gone right out and killed him then if not for Dylan. She told him she'd do it, but she was going to do it her way.

He'd not told her until after the fact what Eddy had done to the children. She would have still killed Eddy, but she might not have been so.... Well, nice wasn't what she was anyway when she'd dealt with him, but Evan figured it was faster. After he told her, she cried for over an hour, then decided that they needed to go shopping for toys and clothing for the family.

Annie was now working for his brother David as his assistant. He'd never had one before and wasn't sure that he really needed one, but after Dylan had a talk with him, he not only hired her on the spot, but had moved the entire family into the apartment he used for writing and started looking for a house. He was as pissed as he'd ever seen him. So was his entire family, as a matter of fact.

The rooms were all nearly done. There were a few things that needed to be finished up, but for the most part the house was completely renovated. He walked into the dining room, the new larger dining room, and loved it. The room now could hold two dining room tables if need be, and the corner cabinets that had been in storage had been cleaned up and filled with their dishes.

Just as he was going out to his car, Dylan and Noreen pulled in. He helped them take in groceries and told her that she'd done well. Noreen snorted and said the rest was coming this afternoon.

"The rest?" Dylan nodded and continued to empty bags. "Dylan, what have you done? And what are we going to need to do to fix it?"

"The council is coming." He nodded. "I want them to like me and not have me brought up before a firing squad. Is that how they'll kill me?"

"No, usually they let the leap tear into you. But I don't think that's anything you have to worry about. Why are they coming here? I thought we were going to them." She told him. "Oh, I see. Okay, that makes more sense. They can talk to Annie and the children under nicer circumstances. But you do know that he had to die."

"Oh yeah, I know that. And even if I knew they were going to put me before a leap of angry tigers, I'd do it the same way. He had to go. And now that I know what he did to those kids, I'd find him and do it all over again. A little slower this time though." Evan knew that about her too. "Also, your family is coming. I thought we could make everyone feel welcome. Then, in the event that they want to murder me, your family will save me."

"Yes, they would. Me too." He kissed her. "I have to go into town for a little while. I have one patient I have to talk to."

"Did you decide to take the job?" He'd had his meeting

with the head of his department, and had been offered the job he'd been wanting forever. "You'd better. I'm going to have enough going on with the president and the leap. I don't need you messing me up."

"I won't. But we're going to have to convert you soon. I don't know how anyone is going to feel about you leading them as a human." She laughed and told him she'd show them. "No more killing, all right?"

She pouted at him and he left her. He wondered if she knew just how sexy he thought her pouting was. Evan was nearly to work when he realized he hadn't answered her. But he was going to take the job. He needed it.

~~~

Sunny moved in and out of the shops, trying to lose the man following her. He was tenacious, she'd give him that. Nodding to Hazel, one of the many people who had helped her over the years, she slipped behind the counter and through the door before the man entered the little stall.

This was the fourth time this week that she'd had to dodge someone coming after her. Either she'd not been as careful as she thought she'd been or they were getting smarter. She doubted it was the latter of the two. For the most part, the goons were as dumb as toast. When Hazel knocked on the door to let her know the coast was clear, she came out.

"You been a bad girl again?" Sunny told her that was all she knew how to do. "Don't I know that? These men, are they the ones that work out at that plant?"

"I think so. I think I might have to take off soon if this keeps up. I'm not nearly as ready as I'd like to be, but I can go now." Hazel told her to wait there for her.

When she disappeared around the door she'd just come out of, Sunny watched the customers. She didn't want to think that everyone was out to get her, but it was true to a point. She'd been having people after her since she was in first grade. More than likely even before that. Hazel came out just as Sunny was beginning to think the man looking at the purses was here for her too.

"Here are the blankets I promised you. And there is some dried meat there too. You keep it dry and you'll have a nice snack." Nodding, she hugged the woman. "You tell me when you land on your feet again. All right? I'll miss you."

"I'll miss you too."

She started to leave but waited until she knew where the purse man was. Stepping into the traffic of people, she was just getting out of the queue when she felt someone behind her. Which was silly, she supposed, since she was in a crowded mall of people and shops. But the feeling was too large to shake and something that she was very used to. Turning at the next right, she found herself at the end of an alley. Before she could turn back, she was cornered.

"Sunshine Davis. How the hell are you?" Not saying anything, she knew she was in deep shit. "I've come to give you a message. To kill you as well, but to tell you why."

"I'm not that easy to kill." He laughed and pulled out a gun. "What is this about? You have some kind of beef with me?"

"I don't. My boss, he does. He doesn't like you snooping around in his businesses. You have been warned. Several times." Sunny tried to think what to do now when the first bullet hit her in the stomach. "Now, I'd like to tell you that you're not going to get anymore to that pretty body of yours, but I know you. You always have ways of getting out of shit."

The next bullet hit her in her arm. She was down now, her body too weak to do much more than just moan. And when he stood over her, she looked up into his face, knowing that if she somehow survived this, she was going to hunt him down.

This bullet was only a distant sound. She wasn't feeling much of anything, so she wasn't surprised that her death would be so lacking in fanfare. Closing her eyes, she let it take her under, sad that she'd not be able to keep her promise to Hazel about keeping in touch.

She woke in bed. Sitting up, she looked down at the wrap on her belly and tried to think what had happened. And where she was. Moving slowly, she made her way to the front and realized that she was in a camper. The kind that you drove as well as slept in.

There wasn't anyone in it with her. No sign that someone had broken into the thing to put her inside. It occurred to her then that she didn't know who she was. Sitting at the table, she tried to think of why she was injured. Who she was as well as where she was headed.

"Something. There's something there." It was too. Like a word on the tip of her tongue, there was a thought there that she couldn't touch. Getting up again, careful of her pain, she found a small sack on the counter and picked it up.

It was a bottle of pills and instructions on how to use them. The handwriting was a fancy script, like something that she'd seen before. Not the handwriting itself, but the script. Setting it on the table, she went to the large fridge and looked inside.

It was well stocked with things like eggs, bacon, and milk. There were lunch meats, tomatoes, as well as a large bag of salad. Small containers of juice that were all unopened. Even the meats were in containers that had plastic wrap around them. The freezer part was equally stocked. Going to the cabinets, she had to rest. Whatever had happened to her, it was extremely painful.

Her head hurt too. Putting her hand to her forehead, she was surprised to find a thick bandage. Finding the bathroom, she stood in front of the mirror and looked at the stranger looking back at her.

The bandage had blood on it, but she ignored that for now. The person in the mirror was no one that she could remember. There were only snatches of things. A gun. A man. There was a woman. The harder she tried to remember, to focus on the faces that flashed before her, the sicker she became. Going back to the bedroom after making sure things were locked up, she realized that she'd have to rest or her head was going to make her unable to think about anything. Grabbing the bag of meds and a bottle of the juice, she sat down.

"Do I take them or not?" The meds were all pain pills; the prescription didn't have a name on it, only a piece of medical tape with the name of the drug on them. All of it was written in the same script as the note had been. Taking the highest dosage that had been mentioned, she lay back on the bed and let them take her under.

When she woke, it was dark in the bedroom as well as outside. Standing slowly, careful of the way she was hurting, she made her way to the bathroom. She found the pills lined up on the counter, as well as another note. Instead of being concerned about the fact that someone had been in the camper with her, she took the recommended dosage again and made her way to the front, taking the note with her.

Opening it up, she looked at the writing and her head spun. She wasn't sick, but there was something there, something that made her want to touch the letters. Laying it on the table, she pressed her palm over it and jerked her hand back.

"What the fuck was that?" She didn't know what she felt, but with trembling hands she laid her hand over it again. "Mother fuck balls."

There was...she wasn't sure what it was, but thought it would be a connection to the person who wrote her the note. She couldn't see his face, but his head bent over the very table she was sitting at as he wrote it. He used a quill and a bottle of ink, and spoke to himself as he did it. Then he looked up, and she had a feeling that he knew she was watching him.

"You must go to Ohio. I don't think you'll survive if you do not get going as soon as possible. Once there, I will visit you in person." She didn't answer him, afraid that if she did, things would get all wonky. "While you rest, I will care for you. But it is important that you leave as soon as possible. You are in grave danger."

"Do you know my name?" He shook his head at her and she felt fear. "Who are you? How is this even possible?"

"I am not here. You are connecting to me in a way that is strange even to me." She told him that wasn't making her feel any better. "Nor myself. I don't care for things that I don't understand. But once you are in Ohio, you will be safe. There are people there, a leap that you can contact and they'll help you."

"Who's after me?" He said that it was someone that she knew. "I don't even know me, how the fuck should I know this person?"

"You will." He stood up then. But instead of walking from the table, his form, his body, was still there too. She looked at him as he stood near her. "You must rest now." Then he touched his fingers to her forehead and her mind closed.

Sitting up in the bed had her crying out in pain. The room was bright with light now. Standing up again, she walked to the bathroom and saw the pills there, but no note this time. Staggering to the kitchen area, holding onto her belly as she went, she looked for the man and anything that might tell her that it hadn't been a dream. That the man, whoever the fuck he'd been, had really been here.

Nothing. There weren't any notes, no indication that anyone but her had been there. There were fresh bottles of pills, this time with typed wording on them, telling her what each of them were and when she could take them. The juice had been replenished as well. Sitting at the table, she tried to make herself think hard on what she knew about anything. All that did was make her ill again.

After she'd dressed, unable and afraid to stand long enough to shower, she decided that she'd get her ass in gear. The same sort of urgency, the one that the man had spoken of, had her sitting at the steering wheel. Touching her hands to it, she felt a tingle, a familiarity that she'd done this before, but didn't dwell on it. Starting her home up, she pulled out of the parking space at a large department/grocery store and pulled into the streaming traffic.

Whoever she was, she was on her way to what she hoped were answers. And she was going to get some of those answers before she did whatever the man wanted of her.

Before You Go...

HELP AN AUTHOR

write a review

THANK YOU!

Share your voice and help guide other readers to these wonderful books. Even if it's only a line or two your reviews help readers discover the author's books so they can continue creating stories that you'll love. Login to your favorite retailer and leave a review. Thank you.

AWARD WINNING, BESTSELLING AUTHOR

Kathi Barton, author of the bestselling series Force of Nature, lives in Nashport, Ohio with her husband, Paul. In addition to writing full time Kathi likes to spend time with her eight grandkids, three children and three children-in-laws. She writes to relax and have fun.

Her muse, a cross between Jimmy Stewart and Hugh Jackman, brings them to life for her readers in a way that has them coming back time and again for more. Her favorite genre is paranormal romance with a great deal of spice. You can visit Kathi online and drop her an email if you'd like. She loves hearing from her fans. aaronskiss@gmail.com.

Follow Kathi on her blog: http://kathisbartonauthor.blogspot.com/

www.ingramcontent.com/pod-product-compliance
Lightning Source LLC
Chambersburg PA
CBHW032128170626
46808CB00006B/2153